Tirzah

Lucille Travis

HERALD PRESS
Scottdale, Pennsylvania
Waterloo, Ontario

Library of Congress Cataloging-in-Publication Data
Travis, Lucille, 1931-
   Tirzah / Lucille Travis.
      p.   cm.
   Summary: Fleeing with Moses from captivity in Egypt, twelve-year-old Tirzah learns a song of hope as she tries to survive to reach the promised land.
   ISBN 0-8361-3546-6
   [1. Palestine—History—To 70 A.D.—Fiction. 2. Jews—Palestine—Fiction.] I. Title.
PZ7.T68915Ti   1991
[Fic]—dc20
                                                      90-23580
                                                         CIP
                                                          AC

The paper used in this publication is recycled and meets the minimum requirements of American National Standard for Information Sciences—Permanence of Paper for Printed Library Materials, ANSI Z39.48-1984.

Scripture is quoted or adapted from *The Holy Bible, New International Version,* copyright © 1973, 1978, 1984 International Bible Society, and used with permission. The Song of Moses (chapter 6 and later references) is from Exodus 15; the covenant-making dialogue (chapter 15), Exodus 19; the Ten Commandments (chapter 19), Exodus 20; the Prayer of Moses (chapters 11 and 17), Psalm 90; and Job's words (chapter 17), Job 19. The events of *Tirzah* are based on accounts in Exodus, Numbers, and Deuteronomy.

TIRZAH
Copyright © 1991 by Herald Press, Scottdale, Pa. 15683
   Published simultaneously in Canada by Herald Press,
      Waterloo, Ont. N2L 6H7. All rights reserved.
Library of Congress Catalog Card Number: 90-23580
International Standard Book Number: 0-8361-3546-6
Printed in the United States of America
Cover art by Mary Chambers/book design by Jim Butti

99 98 97 96 95 94 93 92 91 10 9 8 7 6 5 4 3 2 1

To Jaclyn and Michael,
and Sarah, my young critic

Contents

1

"Why Must You Die?"

Tirzah skirted a small gray lizard and pushed the strap of her goatskin bag further back on her shoulder. At her side Oren worked the wooden crutch under his left arm across a tangle of creeping vines. They were among the thick reeds at the edge of the Nile marsh. Everywhere knives flashed as stacks of dry grasses bound in bundles grew beside their young cutters. Only the children had been spared for the task today.

From behind them someone jeered, "Hey, goat-foot, when are you going to start working?"

Tirzah's hand darted to Oren's bony shoulder, gripping it hard, steering him forward. "It isn't your name," she whispered. "Your name is Oren, and that is all you answer to," she commanded her small brother fiercely.

Oren's face burned a deep red, but he said nothing. Just ahead was a thicket of grasses where they could work out of sight of the rest, and she headed there.

The sun sent down a steady heat in spite of the breeze. Birds hidden in the grasses clicked and chirped, calling noisily. Others clung to the tops of swaying reeds. Oren, his crutch lying nearby, worked on his knees, his crippled foot dragging behind. Tirzah, bending over, worked her way toward him. The sound of running feet made them both look toward the path that led to the road to Succoth.

"Egyptians," she said, keeping her voice low. Oren watched the runners pass, two of them dressed in the loincloths and headgear of the military. "Medjay, from the look of them," he said, "probably after some runaway slave."

Tirzah shook her head as the Egyptian police disappeared from sight. "Whoever it is, I hope they don't find him." Hebrew slave, Nubian, or some poor captive from the Egyptian raids on other countries—it was all the same. They would beat the runaway and return him half-dead to work in the mines or worse. She picked up her knife and bent once more to the grasses.

Oren reached for a clump of reeds and froze. From the thicket that grew high above his head, two dark eyes stared at him. He swung around to grab his crutch and gasped as the form of a man stood up, parting the reeds in front of him.

Tirzah whirled to face them, a handful of grass still in her hand. Startled, she stepped back. The stranger was thin and bony, not an Egyptian from the look of his beardless face. Mud spattered his torn tunic, and bits of grass clung to his hair as he stepped warily into the clearing.

"What do you want?" Tirzah asked, her heart beating fast.

The man turned his empty palms up in a sign of peace. "Nothing. Nothing more than to get out of here in one piece," he said.

From the ground where he still knelt, Oren held his wooden crutch like a shepherd's staff, ready to swing. "You're the one the Medjay were after, aren't you?"

Tirzah turned snapping eyes on her brother, warning him silently to hush.

The stranger looked at Oren for a moment. "Peace, young man," he said. "You are right. Those two would like to have my head. I have done nothing more than any slave would do, given the chance to escape. I ran." A look of cunning crept into his eyes, giving his face an unpleasant hardness. "I am Manetto, an Amorite, slave no more in the Pharaoh's mines."

"The mines?" Tirzah barely whispered the words. It was a rare thing for a slave to escape from the mines except by death.

Manetto's voice was proud. "Yes, the mines, little one. Even there we have heard of your Moses and the god of the Hebrews. When your people go, some of us will leave also. But first I must get out of here," he said, tightening his ragged belt.

Tirzah looked at the swampy marshes from which the stranger had come. "Where will you go?" she asked.

"By now, those sons of donkeys are heading for the road to Megiddo, where they think I will run to escape into the Sinai. But I have no intentions of running further." He looked deeply at Tirzah. "The land of Goshen suits us for now, eh?" With a slight incline of his head, he was off, walking with long strides on the path to the village fields.

As he turned, Tirzah saw his back. Where the rags of his clothing hung in torn strips, marks of the lash crisscrossed in angry, scabbed scars, not yet healed. Her stomach lurched, and she turned away.

Using his crutch to steady himself, Oren stood up. It was always an effort for him to stand. Tirzah bit her lip as she watched him. It was certain that if they did not leave Egypt, Oren would be sent to the fields in the next quota of slaves. The Egyptian taskmasters with their snakelike whips would show him no mercy. Her fingers tightened on the grasses in her hand until they hurt. The Pharaoh must listen to Moses. Yahweh, the Lord God, would make Pharaoh let them go.

"Hey, did you see the fellow's back?" Oren said, breaking into her thoughts.

"Mm," she murmured, stooping to gather a last armful of grass and throw it onto the rest. She didn't want to think of the taskmasters and their whips. Her father and the other slaves would need all the dried grasses they could find to make the bricks Pharaoh demanded. Tirzah straightened her cramped back. The marsh grasses were poor, but they would have to do since Pharaoh refused to give them Egyptian straw.

Fiercely she pressed the top of the load down. Pharaoh was punishing them because he was angry, but he couldn't stop them this time. Oren helped her with the bundle as Tirzah lashed it. They headed back, dragging it between them. By afternoon she had forgotten the slave from the mines.

The house with its thick mud walls and dirt floor was cool. A large, brown scarab beetle, sacred to the Egyptians, scuttled away as Tirzah picked up the waterskin. Quickly she put down the water, stooped, grabbed the bug by its shell, and threw it into the courtyard. Beetles or not, she would miss this little house where she had been born and lived all of her twelve years. But not for a hundred houses would she stay in Egypt. To live free even in the desert would be better. A stab of doubt cut into her thoughts— would Pharaoh refuse to let them go this time?

Oren's low drone above his lessons broke into her thoughts. His crutch was leaning against the wall. Beside it he was sitting cross-legged, his dark head bent over the papyrus on his lap. As he concentrated, a small frown creased his forehead. A dry cough that kept him thin made him pause and look up. Tirzah was used to his coughing, but today the sound nagged her. How would he last in the desert? When he was a baby, she had carried him on her back. He would make it through. She would see that he did.

Crossing the room, she stood above him to look at the papyrus with its strange ink drawings. "You study too much," she said. "What is it you are learning this time?"

"Paser says I can write well enough now, and so he will teach me the stories of Thoth, the bird god." Quickly Oren lowered his eyes, as if fearful of what she would see in them.

Like a darting lizard, Tirzah moved to grip his chin, forcing him to look at her. "How could you listen to teachings about Egyptian gods? Do you want to make Yahweh angry?" Though she didn't do it, she was cross enough to shake the stubborn look from his small boy's face.

"Have you forgotten that it was once the law of Egypt to throw Hebrew boy babies to the crocodile god of the Nile? They would feed *you* to him if Pharaoh didn't need slaves for his fields and mines." Oren's lower lip trembled, and Tirzah released his chin.

"You shouldn't even listen to stories that might anger Yahweh. The gods of Egypt are his enemies." Tirzah looked straight at him, a warning flashing in her eyes. "The Hebrew people have no god but Yahweh."

Oren looked away. "I know, but Paser is a good man," he insisted in a small voice. "He taught me to write. I would insult him by not listening to him these last few days."

Tirzah stamped her foot. "How can you forget that he is an Egyptian? Do you want to be a slave for the rest of your life?"

Oren would not look at her. "Promise me," she said, "you won't listen to any more of old Paser's stories, or I will tell our father, and he will forbid you to see him."

Carefully, Oren rolled the papyrus, reached for his crutch, and struggled to his feet. His brown eyes burned hotly, and he swallowed hard. "You can stop worrying. I'll give the scroll back to Paser," he mumbled.

Tirzah patted his arm, but Oren pulled away. She knew that the old Egyptian scribe treated the lame child like a grandson.

Softening a little she said, "You have to do it, Oren. Here, take the old man a honeycake." Without a word, he took the cake she held out to him. She watched him move to the door, her eyes lingering on the deformed foot.

From the courtyard her mother called impatiently, "Tirzah, where is that water?" Quickly Tirzah poured water from the large clay jug into a small bowl and hurried out. As she stepped from the doorway, for a moment the afternoon sun blinded her eyes. It didn't matter, though. She could have walked the familiar yard blindfolded to where her mother knelt, grinding meal.

Eagerly, her mother reached for the bowl. "Thank you. I feel as if I could never drink enough water these days." Silently, Tirzah watched her drink. Even with dark circles under her eyes, her mother was still young and pretty in spite of a bulging stomach.

"I can do that, Mother, if you want to rest a while." Tirzah knelt and picked some of the husks from the partly ground grain.

Slowly, her mother rose, the folds of her robe falling softly about her prominent stomach. "Promise me that the moment your father and Ram come, you will call me," she said. "They will want their meal."

Tirzah knew. The Egyptian taskmasters kept their slaves working the whole day with only water to keep them going. "I promise," she called. Her mother was already walking toward the house. How will it be, after all these years, to have a new baby in the family? Tirzah mused. Would this one be born lame as Oren had been?

A small green lizard slid away from the shadow of the grinding rock as she worked the stone pestle to crush the grain. Sweat ran down her face, and she stopped to wipe it away. Maybe this time it would be a girl who could help with some of the work.

She finished the last of the grain just in time. "They're coming, Mother," she called. But why was her father leaning on her brother Ram and their uncle Caleb? Between them her father limped as if in pain. Behind her Tirzah heard her mother's sharp intake of breath.

Already neighbors were gathering about the men as Tirzah and her mother ran to them. "What has happened, my husband? What have they done to you?"

Tirzah's father stood as straight as he could. "It is all right, woman, only a beating."

As they helped her father toward the house, Tirzah saw his back. The whip had made long stripes, dark, angry welts caked with blood and dirt. Other lines crossed the first ones, and bits of flesh hung loose. Tears ran down her cheeks, filling her mouth with salt as she followed the procession. Gently, they lowered him face down on a mat.

Turning his eyes from his father, Ram spat. "That Pharaoh. He doesn't listen to reason. How can we make bricks without straw? While we look for it, they taunt us. Today they would not let us use dry grasses without straw. We could not find enough to make our quota of bricks, and you see what they did." Ram raised his fist. "It's all because of that Moses. Ever since he came here, we've had trouble."

His uncle stood and grasped Ram's arm in one huge hand. "You must not raise your hand to Yahweh's chosen, Ram."

Ram lowered his hand and his eyes. "I keep forgetting, Uncle."

"I was young once too, Ram," Caleb said quietly, holding up his well-muscled arms, "and these arms felt the lash more than once."

Ram turned his face to the wall. "But why must we suffer more? Do you think Pharaoh will let us go? Eight times he has pretended to say go."

"Enough, Ram, that's enough." Even from his place on the mat, her father's sharp command made Tirzah jump and Ram stiffen.

A gray shadow of pain crossed his face as her mother applied a wet compress to his back. "You have seen the miracles, Son—the Nile turned to blood, the gnats, the boils—all sent upon Egypt. Have any of us had these things here in Goshen?" He winced as the cloth touched a wound. "Aiee, woman. Ram, you know what I say is true. The Egyptians are feeling the lash of Yahweh's judgment."

Ram said nothing, but Tirzah could feel his anger.

"Look at me, Ram, when I speak," her father commanded. Red-faced, Ram obeyed. "Soon we will leave this place, and not even the Pharaoh of Egypt will be able to hold us back."

"Well spoken." The words rang from a lean, gray-bearded man with the deepest set, clear blue eyes Tirzah had ever seen. He entered with a firm stride.

"Aaron, welcome," her father said. "Tirzah, a drink for our guest."

"No, no, I cannot stay. I have come myself to see how you are, Jeraheel," Aaron said, "and to take a look at your back."

He bent above the wounds, probing gently with his large hands. "So, it is as usual. They do a thorough job," he said. From a small jar he poured oil on the broken skin as he talked. "You have said rightly, Jeraheel. There will be no more slavery for you or any of us. Tomorrow Yahweh will send thick darkness on the land of Egypt."

"The khamsin," her father murmured. "It is that time of year. Without crops to hold down the soil, the wind will tear it away. I dread to think of it." Already the fifty-day wind from the desert blew from the south and southwest. For two or three days each year, it became a great force, picking up sand and dust.

"This will be like no other khamsin," Aaron said. "The Egyptians will not be able to leave their homes. Here in Goshen we are protected and will have light while they sit in darkness."

Wiping the oil from his hands, Aaron looked at Ram. Tirzah saw the question in Ram's eyes just as Aaron must have.

14

Aaron didn't speak directly to Ram, but included them all. "After that Yahweh will send such a thing to Egypt that even Pharaoh will beg us to go," he said. "The last plague will bring death to the firstborn in every Egyptian household from the Pharaoh down."

Her mother gasped, and Aaron looked at her gently. "Yes, Leah, it must be so. Judgment will fall on Egypt's sons if Pharaoh refuses to let Yahweh's children go. Pharaoh has set himself against Yahweh." Aaron shook his head sadly. "You have the lamb ready for sacrifice when the time comes?"

"Yes, everything is as Moses said," her father replied. Tirzah thought of the lamb waiting in the courtyard pen. "Then the time is here," her father said solemnly.

Placing the jar of oil in a small pouch, Aaron nodded. "It has come at last. Now I must go. May the God of Abraham, Isaac, and Jacob reward your faithfulness."

As quickly as he had come, he was gone. Tirzah stood staring at the empty doorway, the cup of water she had fetched still in her hand. When she turned away, Uncle Caleb was smiling at her.

His merry eyes shone as he took the cup in his huge hands. "Yes, little bird, that was Aaron, a man of great strength. May I be as strong as he and Moses when I am that old."

Tirzah laughed. It was well known that Caleb, her father's younger brother, was already as strong as a bull. In one gulp he drained the cup, set it down, and took his leave.

As Tirzah fetched food for their meal, she heard Ram mutter, "Two old men against the Pharaoh. It's madness." Tirzah wanted to shake him for his stubbornness. Instead, brushing past him she gave him her darkest look.

● ● ●

At the house of Paser, the Egyptian, Oren coughed politely and waited. The old man looked up from the roll of papyrus on his lap. "So, young man, it is you. And what brings you here to Paser?"

Paser's faded eyes were gentle, his thin voice kind. Oren sat down awkwardly in front of his friend. "I brought you a honeycake, Paser." He held out the small round cake. "And here is the papyrus you lent me. Our family is going away soon." He stopped, wondering what to say next.

Paser lifted one gnarled, clawlike hand and lightly touched Oren's shoulder. "So, the rumors are true. This Moses, priest of the Hebrew god, will take your people into the desert to hold a feast to your god. But I think you will not come back, eh?" Oren did not answer or move.

Paser withdrew his hand and picked up the honeycake. "Thank your mother for me. She makes a good honeycake." Paser ate slowly, and Oren waited.

At last the old man spoke. "In Goshen we live quietly, Hebrews and a few of us Egyptians, eh? But all over the rest of Egypt, I hear talk of strange things happening because of this Moses. Flies and locusts, hail and sickness, but not in Goshen."

The old man paused, a faraway look in his eyes. Oren sat quietly; he knew that these things were true.

"Perhaps your god watches over his people here in Goshen. Maybe he does not mind old Paser living in the house of my fathers. Like me, it is old, too, eh?" His smile was almost toothless.

"It is a good house," Oren said, looking at the small house with the tall palms beside it.

"We must hurry then, boy, if you are to hear the stories of Thoth before you go." Silently Oren shook his head. "So," the old man said, "you will not come again to Paser for lessons. Perhaps your god does not want to share you with Thoth, eh? No matter. I am an old man. I will sit and dream, and you will grow from a boy to a man. Maybe someday you will think of old Paser who taught you to write, eh?"

Stumbling in his haste, Oren rose and threw his arms about Paser's neck. "I will never forget you, Paser, never."

Gently, Paser freed the boy's arms and gazed into the young face. "When you leave you shall have a present from Paser to take with you. Now go, child, to those who love you and wait for you."

The old man watched the boy go. For a long while he sat staring into the distance. The soft voice of his niece Merrie, calling him for the evening meal, roused him from his dreaming.

As Oren entered the house, Tirzah glared at him. There were no good Egyptians, old or not. She would have nothing to do with Egyptians from now on. Out in the courtyard the yearling lamb began to bleat for his supper, and Tirzah went to feed him.

Her father's orders were to see that nothing happened to the lamb before its time came. The little fellow sprang quickly to her hand, nuzzling it, looking for his food. He was a beauty, perfectly formed.

Poor little thing, Tirzah thought, patting his head. She scratched under his chin. "You are so beautiful, and yet you must die." It was necessary. Moses had given them Yahweh's command to be ready. In every Hebrew home a lamb must be sacrificed on the night that the last judgment fell upon the Egyptians. Its blood would be spread on the doorway. A sign, her father said, that they were trusting Yahweh.

She patted the soft, woolly head, wishing that somehow she could let it escape before it was too late. "I don't understand," she whispered, "why must you die?" Finished with its feeding, the lamb lifted its clear, dark eyes and pressed against her hand.

2

Darkness over Egypt

It was morning, and Tirzah yawned sleepily as she stepped from the house. Instantly she was wide awake. From sky to ground, it looked as if the world had split in two. Like a black wall, thick darkness blotted out the whole of the west where the rest of Egypt should have been. Tirzah stared, wondering at how above her and all of Goshen the sun still shone in the sky. She ran to join her mother and the other women who stood in a small group.

"It is as Aaron said. We have light and they have darkness." Her mother spoke in a voice full of awe. "May it make the Pharaoh believe and let our people go." The threatening blackness hung in the distance like a dark curtain. Tirzah had seen the yearly, dust-filled khamsin wind, but none like this. Surely even Pharaoh would change his mind now.

Ram had come to stand by her. At fifteen he was a head and shoulders taller than Tirzah. For once, he was astonished. "No one can work in that," he muttered.

"Aaron told us so yesterday," Tirzah said smugly. Ram didn't answer. "Admit you were wrong," she coaxed, but Ram shrugged his shoulders and left. Under her breath she muttered, "Brother Donkey." The blackness over Egypt was proof of Moses' words. How she wished she could see behind it.

Hidden by the darkness, the palace of Pharaoh crawled with servants inspecting and filling the lamps that sat or hung everywhere. Windows that should have streamed with sunlight were as black as night. Slaves hurried to bring more lights for the royal family's apartments.

"Eei, the wrath of Seth is upon us," an old woman cried, as she hobbled with her load of fresh linens down the dim hall to her mistress' rooms.

In the courtyard, guards cursed and servants grumbled in the confusion as they carried out their duties by the light of torches. Outside the lamps and torchlight, thick darkness lay in every corner, every window, every hall. It was an unnatural storm, a fearful one. Those on guard duty huddled about their small circles of light, glad for each other's company. Every sound in the surrounding dark made the strongest of them listen nervously.

Thotmes, master bricklayer, quickly heaved the door of his house shut upon the blackness outside. "I have never seen a storm like this. You can feel the dark. It is as if the earth has swallowed up the land." He flung the heavy whip from his hand into a corner, where it lay half-coiled like a black snake. Loosening the belt of his tunic, he slipped out of his sandals.

From her cushions his young wife raised her dark eyes to his. "What will become of us, my husband?" In her arms their firstborn son opened his eyes, and she rocked him gently.

"Nothing will happen if Pharaoh will let the Hebrew slaves go to worship their god." Thotmes sat and reached for the baby. "The land won't take any more. The crops are in ruins, our cattle are sick."

He jiggled his infant son on his lap. "Eh, little one, the

gods are at war. A man cannot fight these things. This time surely Pharaoh will let them go, and good riddance to them, I say." He smiled at the baby, touching its tiny nose with his calloused forefinger, a nose already so like his own.

Back in the palace, in a softly lit room filled with the best furnishings to be found in Egypt, Pharaoh listened to his oldest son. "Father, will you let them go this time? The nobles are worried because they have lost so much grain and cattle."

The boy, a picture of his father, frowned. "I think, Father, that this Hebrew god will not let Egypt alone until his people are allowed to go to the desert and sacrifice to him."

Pharaoh frowned. "Those who complain speak of losses. It is I who suffer when Egypt suffers." Angrily Pharaoh struck his fist against his palm. "Shall the gods of Egypt be mocked by this unknown god?"

The finely drawn black brows on his son's face rose questioningly. "Why do the gods of Egypt allow this unknown god to torment us, Father?"

For a moment Pharaoh was silent. "Perhaps they test us—I do not know, son. I have ordered the priests of Seth to sacrifice three times the amounts required." Pharaoh's eyes grew cold, his mouth grim. "In the end, I will prevail. I will let these slaves go into the desert to worship their god, but they shall leave their flocks and herds here. We shall see how willing they are to go then."

Before him a slave knelt to fasten the royal sandals, and Pharaoh grunted approval of the new design worked in gold across the center strap. Dismissing the slave, he stood up, the royal robe falling in perfect pleats about his tall lean figure.

"You there." The royal finger pointed to one of the Nubian slaves. "Take lamps and see that my house is as bright as the day at once." Turning to his son, Pharaoh's face softened as he took the boy's hand. "Come, let us find your mother. We will make our own light, eh?"

In Goshen the daylight continued. Tirzah, sitting on the ground with an unfinished basket on her lap, glanced at the dark to the west. There was no sign of change. As she reached for another reed, two soft hands covered her eyes from behind. An unmistakable voice said, "Guess who?"

Laughing, Abihail flung herself down beside Tirzah. "Isn't it something?" she said, picking up Tirzah's basket. "The darkness, I mean. At least that Egyptian potter hasn't come around lately. His beady eyes make me shiver." Skillfully she held a new reed as Tirzah attached it to the basket. "Mother makes me hide whenever he comes here. Ugh. I hope he falls into a well in that dark."

"The fat man with the pointed nose?" Tirzah asked.

Abihail nodded, her shining eyes blue as lapis stone. Tirzah pictured the man with just his nose sticking above water and smiled. "Remember when we used to pretend we were Egyptian noblewomen?" she asked.

"Yes, and you even made a little stone god for us to dance before." Abihail bit her lip. "I'm glad no one saw us."

Tirzah's heart skipped a beat. Yahweh must have seen, but it was so long ago. They had been foolish children then. "Not for anything in the world would I be an Egyptian now, even if they do own everything."

Abihail threw her arms wide. "Can you believe we are really going? No more Egypt," she cried, jumping to her feet. Clapping her hands, she twirled in an ancient dance of joy. Slapping the half-made basket against her palm, Tirzah joined in as Abihail whirled.

"Enough," Abihail laughed, stopping to get her breath. "Anyway, I have to get back. Zeruiah is probably calling everywhere for me. Elder sisters are tyrants. You are so lucky not to have one."

She squeezed Tirzah's shoulder lightly and was off. Her long, red hair bounced against her back as she ran. Tirzah pushed a strand of her own black hair away from her face. Abihail was so beautiful. She was better than the sister Tirzah had never had.

A slight noise from behind made her turn. Oren stood leaning on his crutch, looking in the direction Abihail had gone. When his eyes met Tirzah's, she was surprised to see a pink flush spreading over his face. As she looked at him, he lowered his eyes and bent to inspect a sandal strap.

"Well, what is it?" she asked, her swift fingers putting another reed in place. "Have you left Ram with the goats?"

"Yes, and you are to come and help with the packing." He waited while she gathered her reeds for the new basket.

Together they walked through the harvested fields back to the village. Piles of hides, baskets, tents, and rugs lay everywhere. Small children ran and tumbled between and over bundles. Tirzah could feel the excitement in the air. It was all so new. The whole of Goshen was getting ready to leave, and no one who wanted to come would be left behind.

The village street was crowded. She pulled Oren flat against a dried mud wall, out of the way of an old man leading a fat reddish-brown donkey. Though Pharaoh had refused to let the Hebrew people go, they were filtering into Goshen from all over Egypt. Some came by night, others by day, in spite of the watchful eyes of the Egyptian police. Tirzah hadn't dreamed that there were so many of her people. Every house had guests, including theirs.

Under a palm in the courtyard, her mother sorted piles of household goods. Next to her sat the young woman who had come to stay with them. Tirzah shaded her eyes to look, but the woman's twin boys were nowhere in sight.

They will be helping Ram, she thought. She pictured the three of them: Ram, broad-shouldered, straight black hair, square jaw; and the twins, curly-headed like two black sheep, their identical faces thin and dark from the sun. She grinned. Like her, the twins were twelve. Oh, what delicious tricks she would play on Ram if she were a twin.

The woman, Jerioth, was talking to her mother as Tirzah sat down next to them. "It is a fearsome thing to see what has happened to Egypt." Her voice was soft, but her slender hands flew as she talked. "Such thin cattle I never saw, bony and mangy. The Egyptians are terrified. They would not come near us as we fled Thebes."

Her quick fingers paused for a moment. "Some of the women screamed at us to leave Egypt quickly. It was terrible. Only the Pharaoh and his Medjay are hardened against our going. But not even they can keep us now."

Her mother reached a soft hand to Jerioth's brown one. "My dear, I want you to know you are welcome here. I don't know what I would have done without you. But, may I be forgiven, I never thought to see these things happen in my lifetime."

Jerioth looked up, a smile lighting her eyes. "Yes, I know what you mean. My husband, Molid, would repeat the words of the prophecy his father said to him and his grandfather before that." Lifting her head she recited the ancient saying of Joseph. "Yahweh will surely take care of you, and you will carry my bones up from here."

Jerioth looked thoughtful for a moment. "Still, it seems like a dream, doesn't it? Moses has said that long ago in the time of Abraham, Yahweh foretold that his people would go up from Egypt after four hundred years. Think of it, Leah, this very year is the four hundredth year since our people first came to Egypt."

From the crowded street a voice called a greeting. Tirzah turned to look as her mother waved briefly. "That one," her mother said, "is my brother Shobal."

Tirzah waved and smiled at the short, stout man, her uncle Shobal, hurrying past them. Once he had given her a necklace with a worked stone. Poor Uncle Shobal. He was not well loved at her house. He and her father never agreed on anything.

Her mother shook her head. "From the time he opened his eyes, our Shobal was trouble. Since the day Moses arrived, Shobal argues and argues, demanding proofs from Moses, even blaming him for Pharaoh's cruelties."

"Will he go with us when the time comes to leave?" Jerioth asked, brushing an ant from Tirzah's lap. Tirzah smiled her thanks.

"That one? He will go with us because to stay behind is too risky. Shobal is a practical man," her mother answered, sitting back on her heels. Good, Tirzah thought, because that meant Shobal's family would travel with them, and that meant Abishur would come. He was handsome, gentle, fifteen, and not at all like his father, Shobal. Among the eligible young men, Abihail preferred him above all the other possible future husbands she and Tirzah could imagine.

"Come," her mother said, rising. "Time to pack the tent."

Tirzah was on her feet instantly. The new goatskin tent would be their desert home! To the west the darkness still hung thick and heavy over the land as she followed her mother into the house.

Three days later the darkness lifted, and Pharaoh summoned Moses. On his throne Pharaoh sat splendidly arrayed in the finest of linen embroidered with gold. On his forehead a gold serpent with a jeweled eye flashed as he inclined his head.

Before the court stood two men, one tall with a full white beard, his skin and clothing that of a Bedouin. Pharaoh briefly glanced at the other, a lean, gray-bearded man. It was the tall one with the piercing eyes, the one called Moses, that drew him like a magnet. The man's eyes seemed to burn in his sun-darkened face, and Pharaoh turned away slightly in spite of his will to outstare this one.

Breathing deeply, Pharaoh let his hatred of this man fill

him until every muscle was taut. When he spoke, his words were hard as iron. "Go, worship your god. Your women and children may go with you, but your flocks and herds will stay here." Behind him the royal scribe murmured a soft sound of approval. A small proud smile turned the corners of Pharaoh's mouth upward as he watched the men before him, disappointment clear on their faces. He waited for Moses to give his answer.

Bowing low, Aaron stepped forward. "May Pharaoh live long, but you must allow us to have sacrifices and offerings to the Lord our God. Our livestock must go with us. Not a hoof is to be left behind. We do not know until we get there what we must use in our worship of Yahweh."

Pharaoh was on his feet instantly. "Do you think I am a fool? I will hear no more of this. None of you shall leave Egypt." Pharaoh raised his arm, his hand a tight fist. "Get out of my sight!" he shouted. "And do not appear before me again! The day you see my face you will die." Turning his royal back, he moved toward the curtained doorway, signaling that court was over.

Before anyone could follow, the voice of Moses rang out. "This is what the Lord says: About midnight I will go throughout Egypt. Every firstborn son in Egypt will die, from the firstborn son of Pharaoh, who sits on the throne, to the firstborn son of the slave girl, who is at her hand mill, and all the firstborn of the cattle as well."

No one moved or spoke as Moses continued. "From all over Egypt there will go up a great cry, the like of which has never been heard before, nor ever will be again. But throughout all Israel no sound will be heard from man or beast, not even a dog's bark."

Moses turned his eyes upon the group of nobles standing in stunned amazement. He raised his rod toward them. "All these officials of yours will come down to me, bow down before me, and cry, 'Go away, you and all the people who follow at your heels.' When that time comes, I shall go." His face burning with anger, Moses turned his back to the court and with Aaron strode swiftly from the palace.

Outside the sky was clear, the warm, golden sun shining once more. Moses walked on in silence. Aaron glanced behind them. No one had followed them.

When at last Moses spoke, it was to Aaron's surprise. "You must tell the leaders of every clan that they are to see that men and women alike ask their Egyptian neighbors for articles of silver and gold to take with them. Yahweh wills it." Puzzled, Aaron looked at Moses. But before he could ask anything, the sound of running feet made them both turn to look back.

An Egyptian servant, one belonging to an upper-class family from the look of his clothes, hurried toward them and bowed low. "My lords, I am sent by the household of noble Sesostris to bring you this small gift." The man held out a box of carved wood and opened its lid for them. Inside the box were four gold ibises, each tiny bird perfect. Aaron took the box in his large hands.

"You must thank your master for us," Moses said.

As they went on, Moses murmured softly, "What do you think, Aaron, could these gold ibises be the wages of some Hebrew slave for a lifetime of slavery?"

"As you say, Moses, it may be that Yahweh will see to it that the Egyptians pay their laborers indeed," Aaron said. He hurried to match his brother's stride. Once again Moses grew silent, and Aaron made no more comments.

After a while Moses began to talk, his face grim. "Aaron, we must remind the people. None are to set foot outside their houses this night until the signal to march is given. You will slay the lamb for our house, brother?"

Aaron nodded. All was ready.

Without slowing his pace, Moses gripped Aaron's arm. "Not one thing must be forgotten." His voice was tense as he repeated the instructions. "Everything must be done exactly as Yahweh has said. This will be a night Israel shall never forget, and one Pharaoh will rue for the rest of his days."

Once more Moses fell silent. Aaron too was quiet. The night ahead of them would be unlike any other.

3

"Go and Do Not Return"

Oren worked his crutch in the peculiar rhythmic way that allowed him to go quickly on the narrow path. He could not remember a time without a wooden crutch, though he had outgrown many of them. Squinting his eyes against the glare of the sun, he saw Paser sitting under the fig tree, reading from a papyrus scroll.

Paser looked up, a half-formed word on his lips. "Is it time, boy? Time for old Paser to wish you well on your journey?"

Oren nodded.

"Well then, go into the house and fetch the bundle by the door. You cannot miss it—go ahead."

Oren turned toward the house, its door open to the air. On the dirt floor just inside the doorway was a small skin bag with leather thongs. Lifting it, he saw that its strap would fit nicely about his neck. It was not heavy.

Outside in the shade Paser motioned him to sit on the little wooden stool at his feet.

"I thank you, Paser for the gift," Oren said. "Shall I open it?"

"Not now, boy. It will keep. Wait until you have gone one day's journey. It will be a small pleasure to look forward to."

Oren nodded. "Paser, I have something to ask you." Oren cringed at what he must say. "Today my father will kill the yearling and put its blood on the doorposts and lintel of our house. Not just our house. Every Hebrew family must do the same. Tonight none are to leave their house or they will die."

Paser did not move or speak, and Oren went on. "Moses says. . . ." Oren felt his mouth grow dry and the words he wanted began slipping away.

All at once they came tumbling out. "Tonight the first-born in every Egyptian household will die, the flocks and herds, too. Paser, please come home with me to our house. My father will not turn you away. Already some Egyptians have begged their Hebrew neighbors to let them go with them. Please, Paser, come with us. I will teach you about Yahweh. Paser?"

Paser bowed his bald head. When he finally looked up, it was not at Oren, but at something far away. With a small sigh the old man brushed off a fly and turned his eyes to Oren. "I have lived many years in my father's house. I should like to die here. You and I, we can do nothing about the powers that rule our lives."

The fly returned to land on Oren's arm and Paser stopped to flick it away. "I will offer a gift to your god Yahweh to-night. But this is where I belong." Paser looked about him at the mud-brick house, the garden, then back at Oren. "You must go with your people, and I must stay with mine."

Now it was Oren who bowed his head and wept while the old man crooned soothingly, trying to comfort him.

• • •

In the late afternoon Tirzah returned to the house, holding her clenched hands close to her chest. "Mother, look what Ahmose, the Egyptian, gave us to wear on our journey." In her outstretched hands lay two necklaces of thin beaten gold with tiny blue stones laced among the strands.

Tirzah stared at her mother and Jerioth. "I didn't want to go there and ask her for ornaments because I thought she would get angry, but she didn't. She gave me the necklaces and said she hoped they would please our God."

Jerioth's hand went to the silver beads around her own neck. "This too was a present from an Egyptian woman," she said. "She was a stranger, and yet she forced the necklace into my hand, begging me to wear it before our God." Jerioth's large doe eyes glistened softly. "I was sorry for that woman, really sorry."

Slowly, Tirzah let the gold chains slip through her fingers into her mother's hand. "I suppose I cannot wear one?" she asked, her voice lifting with hope.

"No, you cannot. Time enough when you are betrothed." Tirzah wanted to beg, but she knew it was hopeless. Her mother had strict ideas of what was proper for a young girl.

"Did you remember to wrap the bread trough?" her mother asked.

"Yes, Mother," Tirzah said, looking about at the bare walls, the empty shelves. Against the far wall stood the packs each would carry. Only a bundle of rushes and the things they would need for this night's supper remained unpacked.

The rushes, her mother had said, were to sweep the house one last time before they left. She would not leave it dirty for whoever might come after them. Who would come to live here? Tirzah wondered. Slaves captured from another land, perhaps. Or would the house just stand empty forever?

By evening the smell of roast lamb filled the room. It was

hot inside the small house, crowded with those who had joined Tirzah's family for the meal. She longed for a breath of cool night air. The door was shut tight against the terrible thing that was coming. Would she hear it? Not for anything would she go outside that door marked with the lamb's blood.

Next to her sat old Hanna, her strong hands resting on her lap. A smile crossed the wrinkled folds of her face. "Eh, little one, this is a night to remember. These eyes never thought to see our deliverance from Egypt."

She paused and took Tirzah's hands in her gnarled brown ones. "You, child, will live in a land of milk and honey and have many children, all of them free."

Tirzah nodded, rather than shout at the old woman who was getting deafer than ever.

Hanna patted Tirzah's hand. "You mustn't be afraid, child. We are safe in here with the blood of the lamb your father put on the doorposts." The old woman coughed and released her grip on Tirzah's hand.

Taking the opportunity to escape, Tirzah excused herself and made her way to a place beside Oren against the far wall. Oren's eyes were closed, his thin face pale. All evening he had said nothing. As she sat beside him, he opened his eyes, then closed them again.

He will make himself sick, she thought, if he doesn't stop mourning for the Egyptian Paser. Maybe the old man wasn't an eldest son in his house and wouldn't die. She wanted to shake Oren and make him understand. It was Pharaoh's own fault if his people died.

Outside, the wind blew around the house, a mournful, uneasy sound. A cold shiver ran down her arms in spite of the warm room. What was happening out there? If only Pharaoh had listened to Yahweh—but now it was too late. Across the room their neighbor Ezri, bent and white-haired, talked to her father. Poor Ezri. Tirzah thought of his two sons who had died in the dreaded copper mines.

Oren still sat with his eyes closed. Under her breath, low enough for just Oren to hear, she whispered, "If Yahweh didn't make Pharaoh let us go tonight, one of these days you would be sent to the fields or maybe the copper mines like Ezri's sons." The small flicker of one eyebrow let her know he had heard.

Tirzah closed her own eyes and found herself wondering about the runaway Amorite they had met in the marshes. He was probably safe inside the house of a Hebrew family somewhere in Goshen, its door like theirs outlined in lamb's blood.

She opened her eyes and looked at her father talking quietly with the men. She was glad he had done what Moses commanded. Yahweh would see and know they were obeying him, and they would be safe.

Her mother's voice startled her. Oren poked her ribs, and Tirzah wondered, had her mother called her more than once? The meal was ready, the lamb at the center, bowls of bitter herbs and unleavened bread placed around it.

Her father, Molid, old Ezri, Ram, the twins, and Oren stood together, the men with their staffs in their hands. Molid, Jerioth's husband, was a short, wiry man with thick, curly hair like that of his twin sons. Tirzah stood next to old Hanna with the women and waited for her father to say the blessing.

"On this night we give thanks," her father began. Tirzah's mind wandered to the world outside of the house, and she heard no more. What could be happening out there? What awful judgment was about to pass over their house? With a shiver she pressed her eyes closed tighter and tried to listen to the words of the prayer.

Solemnly, her mother served the bitter herbs to each of them. Tirzah took her portion and ate it in little bites along with the meat. It was not as bad as she thought; the bitter mix slid down easily. Nothing must be left of this special lamb, and her mother had guessed right. There was just enough food for the number of people at their meal.

After they finished eating, the men sat talking in their corner of the room. Tirzah, her eyes heavy, slumped by Jerioth, watching her quick fingers knot the fringes of a belt.

Somewhere in her dreams, mixed with the sounds of feet moving and donkeys braying, something was shaking her awake. It was her mother's hand gripping her shoulder, her excited voice saying, "Come, it's time to go."

Suddenly Tirzah remembered. Had she missed it all? The thing out there, had it come and gone while she slept?

From the open doorway she could see the light of the full moon—it was still night. She had missed it. Why did she have to be a person who slept like a brick the moment her eyes closed?

Stumbling over bundles that were everywhere on the floor, she made her way into the courtyard. The road was alive with people and animals. She recognized her uncle's family, and a little way back her mother's brother Shobal and his family. The whole clan was gathered to march together. This was it, the day to be like no other, the day of all days.

"I'm coming, I'm coming," she shouted, running to help her mother and Jerioth carry bundles to Ram and her father.

"This excuse for a donkey hasn't sense enough to hold still," Ram complained, while Tirzah grinned at the little, reddish-brown donkey her father had named Sorry. Once more Ram approached the donkey and spoke harshly to it.

"You miserable creature, hold still." As he spoke he pulled tightly on the strap binding the heavy load. Instantly Sorry swerved, barely missing him with her hind feet.

Tirzah, near the donkey's head, stepped back out of the way of Sorry's big teeth. It was Ram's fault that he could never get along with the donkey. Only one thing meant peace

33

with Sorry, and Tirzah felt in her belt pouch for it. Carefully, slowly, she held the sweet cake out toward the donkey.

"What she needs is a good beating," Ram said, lifting another bundle onto the donkey's back. "You spoil her."

Tirzah was about to accuse him of pulling the thongs too tight when she saw his face. Dark circles lined his eyes as if he had not slept at all. The rest of his face was pale. Had he seen it, the thing that had come while she slept? He was scared, and she knew it. He was also angry, and he turned his back to her questioning look.

By the time they began to move, Tirzah found herself assigned to a place in the strict line of march. She could not see Abihail or leave to find her. For that matter, in spite of the full moon that touched everything with soft brightness, she could see little either in front of her or in back, except for the donkeys piled high with bundles. On either side of her was a wall of people. It was as if a feast-day crowd had suddenly grown until it covered the land solid with people.

In her own place in this living, moving mass, she walked with her cousins, all of them near her age. They pressed close, and Tirzah was glad for their company in the strange night that covered everything outside the light of the torches.

Nahalath, the oldest of them, her long lashes dark against her pale skin, looked as if she hadn't slept. She was tall, and Tirzah thought she was as beautiful as a delicate water lily.

Maacah, next to her, had plaited her thick black hair into a braid the width of Tirzah's two arms. Stouter and not as tall as Nahalath, Maacah wasn't pretty until she smiled. She smiled now as Tirzah offered her a piece of unleavened bread to nibble.

Rachel, the youngest cousin, tripped over a loose stone, and Tirzah helped her up. "Thanks," Rachel said, pushing back strands of limp reddish-brown hair from her eyes. She was always bumping into something. Her thin bony arms

34

and legs were usually spotted with bruises.

Tirzah shook her head. The girls had tried fixing Rachel's hair in a tight braid, adding color to her belt, helping her drape her mantle. But she remained skin-and-bones Rachel, with feet too large for the rest of her. A dried flower had fallen from Rachel's belt, and Tirzah picked it up quickly, holding it for a moment to breathe its fragrance. This was Rachel's specialty. Whatever grew—herbs, flowers, wild plants—she knew them all.

Handing the blossom back to Rachel, Tirzah murmured, "Nice." She hadn't noticed it before, but the night was full of odors like a roomful of people, animals, and burning torches.

How long they had been walking, Tirzah didn't know. Dawn broke first with gray streaks at the edge of the sky, then pink, and suddenly morning light. As the sun rose, she could tell they were moving southeast.

With daylight came the deep, wailing sounds of Egyptians mourning their dead on the way to the burial grounds. As a funeral procession with its low-throated drums drew nearer, Tirzah could not see it at first. Silently the marchers halted, and through the gaps between the lines she saw it.

Behind the biers Egyptian men followed weeping, and after them the women walked, beating their breasts and crying. One woman was clinging to a small, cloth-draped body being carried on a litter. Suddenly she raised her arms above her head and cried out, "Go, oh, go quickly to your Hebrew god and do not ever return."

Immediately other Egyptians near her joined in begging them to leave quickly. Tirzah wanted to cover her ears from the awful sounds. As the procession passed, the march began again, and Tirzah hurried on away from the drums and cries.

Just ahead, her mother rode on a mule with Jerioth walking beside her. Oren, who had stubbornly refused to ride, walked by their cousin, Abishur. Gradually the sound of drums faded, and the noise of voices and animals filled the air once more.

Abishur took out his flute and played a song for Oren as they walked. While he played, the folds of his tunic opened a little—enough for Tirzah to notice the short sword belted to his waist. How had he come by a sword, and why was he wearing it?

Tirzah's eyes swept the figures of the men in front of her, seeing for the first time that some wore a sling of arrows and carried their bows on their backs. Others wore swords or long knives in their belts, and a few carried spears. Though she knew her father owned a long knife, he had never worn it in public. Slaves were not usually armed. But now they were leaving Egypt, and everything was changed.

She thrust her shoulders back, lifted her chin, and walked as she had seen the leaders of grand Egyptian processions walk—proud and free. Overhead the sun climbed higher, warming her and shining on everything around her. Somewhere the Promised Land waited. It was all like a wonderful dream, and she was part of it.

Abishur hoisted Oren to his shoulders, and Oren looked back to wave his crutch at her, narrowly missing Abishur's ear. Tirzah winced, then laughed. A warm feeling filled her, love for Oren, Abishur, and even Ram walking up ahead. She felt glad all over.

It did not last long. As the morning wore on, the funeral drums began again, more and more of them. The sounds of wailing cries chilled her in spite of the sun.

4

The Trap

At last they halted for the night near Succoth.

Tirzah's legs felt stiff and heavy, her hands swollen, and her mouth dry from the long hours of march. She was hungry and covered with fine dust.

"Come on," Maacah urged, half supporting Nahaloth, who leaned heavily on her arm, her veil draped across her mouth.

"Not another step could I go. I can't make it," Nahaloth wailed as Maacah pulled her. "If only I could sink my feet into cool Nile mud just for one hour," she grumbled.

"That's a dumb thing to say," Maacah scolded, keeping a steady pull on her sister's arm. "Just don't let Father hear you say a word about Egyptian mud."

"Mud is mud," Nahaloth answered, "and right now I'd give anything for one pot of it."

Tirzah grinned as she pictured Nahaloth's feet stuck in a pot of mud. Now that she was standing still, she began to feel little stabs of muscle pain in her own legs. Pushing one foot ahead of the other, she made her way to where her mother and Jerioth were already unpacking the tent.

It was Jerioth who took charge. Her wide smile greeted Tirzah while her nimble fingers coaxed a flame to life. Tirzah undid a packet of goat's curd, glancing as she did at her mother, who rested against a pile of bundles. Her eyes were closed, her face drawn and pale with fatigue.

Silently, Jerioth put a finger against her own lips, and Tirzah nodded. Once her mother woke, but Jerioth smiled and insisted, "Close your eyes, Leah. Rest for the baby's sake. Let me take care of the meal."

The food was ready, and Tirzah was hungry. But still the men had not returned from their meeting with Moses and the leaders. When they did come, it was her uncle Shobal's voice she heard first.

"Can't you see that the only safety is in speed?" her uncle was saying in a firm tone. "We must go northeast and take the way toward Megiddo, the quickest route, the one we know is direct to Canaan. Jeraheel, you are a man of good sense. You know that to go to Etham will take us further away from the main road."

Her father threw his staff on the ground. "That is all quite clear, but one thing you forget. Moses is the one God has spoken to, and he says we go to Etham."

Her mother opened her eyes, and the men lowered their voices. "Besides," her father said, "the Egyptians keep the forts and guard stations along the main coastal route well manned. The road is shorter, but might lead straight into war."

"That's a risk we have to take," argued Shobal. "It would be sheer folly to go wandering around in that rough country when every hour between us and Pharaoh's army counts. Hasn't the Pharaoh proved he is one whose mind changes with every breeze?"

Shobal turned away, gesturing to a handful of men who stood nearby listening. "Come, let's not waste our time. There are others who will listen to reason."

Tirzah watched the men leave and wondered. Was it possible that the Pharaoh would send his army after them? She looked questioningly at her father. He was not tall, but he was muscular, his fingers strong as he kneaded her shoulder gently.

"Child, never mind Shobal. Moses has brought us this far, and we must trust in Yahweh's chosen to lead us the rest of the way."

He flashed a weary smile at her, and Tirzah felt warm inside. Her father's word was good enough for her.

A cool evening wind sprang up, smelling of night things, mysterious and strange under the star-brilliant sky. Not for a long time had Tirzah noticed the stars. These were large, so bright, almost like a covering above the camp, stretching as far as she could see. She was glad not to be inside the tent tonight, glad too that she hadn't fallen asleep yet.

Next to her, Oren lay stiff and silent. "Are you awake?" she whispered, knowing that he was.

"Yes." The answer came in a small hard voice. All day he had insisted on walking, until Abishur had carried him. Later Tirzah's father had made him ride in the cart with old Hanna and the little ones to practice the flute and cheer the children who were restless.

"Oren, are you in pain?"

"Why should I be?" He gritted his teeth on the half-lie. Tomorrow he would grit them again, and the day after that.

"Oren, look at the stars. The signs are good. See how they line up, almost like a shining pathway, as if they were showing us the way to the new land." She sighed, thinking of the land that waited for them. Who lived there now? What would the houses be like? She would plant a garden first thing.

"Oren, did you hear Father say that Yahweh planned this journey a long time ago? Those same stars shone on Joseph hundreds of years ago. Maybe on the night he made his children vow to take his body with them when they left Egypt."

"I know," Oren mumbled. "I saw Aaron and the others carrying the box with Joseph's bones inside." Oren was silent, remembering the sight of the draped coffin. How he would love to see inside that box.

"Oren," Tirzah murmured, "think of it—no more Egypt. We're free." She could hear her own voice growing sleepier.

Oren turned his head away and looked up at the sky. He was free, but why did part of him still feel like it was missing? Was Paser alive? Had Yahweh accepted his sacrifice? He looked hard at the stars trying to see behind them.

Silently he prayed. "Lord, will you have mercy on old Paser? He was good to me, and I can't help it—I, I love him." Tears wet his cheeks and cooled in the breeze as he closed his heavy eyelids.

In the morning the ram's horn sounded once more, echoing throughout the camp from tribe to tribe, calling the people to gather. "Another day in the sun," Tirzah grumbled. She could feel the heat already.

Maacah had pinned her thick black braid into a coil above her neck and caught one of the pins in her head covering. Sweat dripped from her nose as she struggled to free the cloth. "At least the afternoon will be better with the sun behind us," she said, sighing as the knot of braid loosened. "Ooph, there will be nothing left of me by the time we reach the new land."

Tirzah hid a smile, looking at Maacah's round, red face and plentifully filled robe.

Nahalath laughed at her sister. "Mother says the new land is filled with milk and honey, so I suppose, Maacah, it will not hurt you to lose a little weight before we get there."

Tirzah glanced down at her own skinny frame, her robe covered with fine dust. Dust was everywhere. She shook her skirt and brushed away the little cloud that rose from it. Turning to escape the dust, she faced east for the march to

Etham. In the sky was the strange white, cloudlike mass that had hung there ever since dawn. It was huge, almost silvery white, as if it were filled with light.

"What could it be, Tirzah?" Maacah asked in a hushed voice.

Behind the girls, Jerioth's voice spoke. "Molid says it is the presence of Yahweh. He has come to guide us on our journey."

While they watched the huge cloudlike column, it seemed to Tirzah that it moved. As she stared, the cloud did move. It was leading them—going ahead of them. Tirzah clapped her hands and laughed. The cloud was going toward Etham. Her father was right, and Uncle Shobal would have no choice but to admit it.

When the cloud stopped, the long line of march halted for rest and food. When the cloud moved on, the people moved on. "Nothing like this has ever been in this world before," Tirzah whispered to herself. But by the time the cloud stopped for the night, she was dusty, weary, and aching in every muscle.

Etham, on the edge of the desert, was beautiful, with palm trees and wells. When it was her turn at the well, Tirzah filled her waterskin quickly. How clear the water looked as it splashed into the goatskin. She drew enough for the family and hurried back to the campfire, glad that Oren would care for the goats and sheep.

Lazily, Tirzah bit into one of the sweet dates that clustered on the palms. She let it linger on her tongue a while before she swallowed it. From where she sat, she could see little circles of fire like theirs dotting the horizon.

In the east the cloud of mystery hovered like a burning red-gold column that seemed to fill that part of the night. She could barely turn her eyes from it. It was like a glorious sunset that didn't die away or go down. Tirzah sighed for the wonder of it.

Her mother's commanding voice broke into her thoughts. "Come, Oren, let me see those feet of yours. Why didn't you ride with Hanna in the cart? Why must you insist on walking so much?" Her mother was inspecting Oren's lame leg, and Tirzah bit her lip as Oren flinched.

"What should a mother do with such a stubborn son? Tirzah, bring me the ointment from the medicine pack." As she spoke she massaged the thin leg between her hands. When Tirzah brought the jar of ointment, her mother looked at her with eyes that barely held back the tears shining in them. Hastily, she took the ointment and set about briskly rubbing the leg. Oren gritted his teeth, and Tirzah turned away.

Carefully she fed a stick into the fire. The night was not yet cold, but she knew it would be. As she bent over the low flames, hurrying feet and angry voices broke the stillness of the night. Her father strode into the firelight, Ram behind him.

"But Father, can't you see that to turn back now and go toward the Reed Sea will put us between the sea and the mountains? It makes no sense at all. We should have headed for the coastal highway long ago," Ram pleaded.

Tirzah listened for the reply.

"Moses has spoken tonight, saying we go south from Etham, and so we go south. Don't I know that the sea and the wilderness are there? And doesn't Yahweh, may he be praised, know what he means to do?"

Her father, loud when he was angry, raised his voice. "No son of mine will question the chosen of God. You have been listening to that donkey of a Shobal. He has put these ideas in your head." Stomping into the tent, her father dropped the black, goatskin curtain door behind him.

Ram slumped heavily by the campfire, his face grim. "Insane," he muttered, "a madness to turn south and be hemmed in like sitting birds for the hunter."

"But what about the cloud of Yahweh? Won't it go before

us to show us the way?" Tirzah asked.

"Who knows," Ram answered, jabbing at the dying coals of the fire. "Surely Yahweh expects us to show reason and good sense. Moses is old. How can he be certain he is leading in the direction Yahweh is pleased with? What if the cloud only goes before us to test our foolishness? It makes no sense at all to walk into a trap. How can this be of Yahweh? Can a foolish thing be from Yahweh?"

Tirzah shivered from the night air and from something inside. What if Ram was right? The shortest route to the land of Canaan was along the coast, but they were far from that now. On the other side of Shur was a rough track going east through the wilderness. Instead they were turning south. Were they lost? No, that made no sense. Why then, was everything so complicated, so hard to understand?

Already the others were gone to their beds. A heaviness began to press down on Tirzah's eyes as she pulled her cover close. At the campfire, Ram still sat staring into the glowing coals. What if he is right? Tirzah wondered. Maybe in the morning, the cloud would not turn south. That would be good, she thought.

The day dawned bright and hot. When the marchers again took their places, Tirzah saw that the cloud had moved toward the south. Slowly the line began its march in that direction.

Why, oh, why was Yahweh letting them go away from the route to Canaan into what might be a trap?

5

The Bottom of the Sea

Ram whacked his staff across Sorry's rump as she slowed almost to a standstill. "Move on, you excuse for a donkey," he yelled. Sorry bared her teeth menacingly at Ram as she began walking, the load of bundles swaying. "As I was saying, Jonathan, your father is right. Something has to be done."

Even as he spoke, Ram felt confused. The whole plan of escape was turning into a nightmare. On a nearby rock a dabb lizard, its green body spotted with brown, slipped quickly into a crevice and out of sight.

"Right, but what do we do next?" Jonathan's thick black eyebrows rose in pointed arches just as his father Shobal's did when he was thinking through a matter. "Look here, Ram, if we get enough men on our side, then the rest will have to go along or split the camp."

The idea of a split camp made Ram's stomach burn. What would he do when his father chose the other side? For his father would surely do so, as sure as the desert held sand.

Jonathan held up one hand, counting on his fingers as he spoke. "For one thing, we know the rabble group that joined us to get themselves away from the Egyptians aren't going to stick with this route much longer. Already that Amorite Manetto, the one from the mines, is going around grumbling."

Ram nodded his head. He had noticed the man, an Amorite of mixed blood with a cold, cruel smile. Long purple scars crossed and crisscrossed the fellow's back, and no one had questioned his desire to leave Egypt.

"My father says there are at least fifty men in every tribe solidly opposed to this plan of Moses. You can add to that hundreds of others just waiting for some good leadership." Jonathan's voice fell to a whisper, and he placed his left hand on Ram's arm. "Ram, your father will just have to go along with the rest of us when the time comes."

Ram nodded. He knew that Jonathan was wrong, though, that nothing short of the voice of God would change his father's mind. Even if he could make his mother listen, she couldn't change his father. She would stick with him, too, no matter what price they all had to pay.

Ram could feel the sun beating down through his head cover, and still the cloud that went before them made no sign of stopping. Nothing made sense. Why were they hurrying, marching on and on away from the promised land? Why couldn't they at least stop for food? He was hungry, thirsty, and yes, angry.

When the white cloud stopped at last, it rested over a wide plain that lay between rugged hills rising like walls on the west and south. To the east was a papyrus marsh, and beyond that, the Sea of Reeds. Lush green grasses waved in the breeze. But except for the way they had entered, there was no way out of the plain. All of Ram's fears had come true. Blue waters sparkled in the sun as far to the east as Ram could see, and the air was sweet with the smell of it, but Ram felt no gladness at all.

At the edge of the water, Nahalath twisted her long

brown hair into a knot. Kicking off her sandals, she waded in to join Tirzah, who was already knee-deep in the shallows. Tirzah let her hands trail beneath the surface, wriggling her fingers like small white fish. All around her people were standing in the water, laughing and talking. Children splashed each other happily. It was as if this were the promised land, and they had arrived.

Out of breath, Maacah, her face redder than ever, joined them. "Oh, that feels good," she said. "Do you know, Tirzah, I could stay right here forever. Just think how lovely it would be to live by the shore."

"Yes, and the mountains," Tirzah said, straightening her body and looking back at the hills circling the plain like sleeping giants. She wouldn't mind camping here for a long time. Maybe the cloud of God had hurried them here just for that.

Jerioth made the meal, a delicious broth of dried onions and herbs whose smell made the mouth water. Tirzah sat cross-legged, listening to the sounds that carried so clearly here on the plain. She could hear her uncle Shobal's voice raised in argument.

Her mother, hearing it too, was cross. "Not again! Will that brother of mine never stop?" In the little crowd of men standing by Shobal's tent, Tirzah made out her uncle, gesturing wildly as he talked.

The voices of a number of the men rose in loud shouts of "No," and then, "Unite, we say." They were drawing attention, and others were joining them. Tirzah couldn't hear above the noise, but suddenly there was a hush as two men made their way to stand on a great outcrop of rock facing the people. It was Moses and Aaron. Moses lifted his hand for silence.

"Listen to me." Moses' voice seemed to Tirzah to be right next to her, it was so clear. "Yahweh is leading us, and this is the way he has chosen for us to go. You must not turn away to your own route or you will be lost. Yahweh will fulfill his promise to lead us to Canaan."

From the listening crowd, Tirzah heard her uncle's voice cry out, "How can this be the way to Canaan? Are we to go through the sea, or over the mountains, or back the way we came?" Other shouting voices joined in: "Back the way we came. Back before it's too late."

Angry voices raised above the first ones shouted, "We are with Moses and Yahweh. We follow the Glory." Soon a chorus of loud voices chanting, "Follow the Glory," drowned out the protesters. When it was over, Moses dismissed the people and went back to his own campfire.

Tirzah's eyes burned with staring, and her voice was hoarse from crying, "Follow the Glory." She had stood with her father, and together they walked back to their site. Oren was there with Jerioth, her mother, and the twins, but Ram was nowhere in sight.

Her father went straight to her mother and held her close. "It will be all right, my love," he said. "Something good will come from following this route. Yahweh will guide us."

"I was so afraid there would be a split in the camp, but what you say is true. Something good will come of it. I am ashamed to be related to that Shobal." Her mother stood back, a fire kindling in her eyes. "I'm of a mind to tell him what I think."

Tirzah smiled as her father laughed his deep from-the-toes-up laugh. "Look, Tirzah, what have we here? A lioness ready to eat up that mouse Shobal? We are lucky she doesn't growl at us."

"Lioness, am I? We shall see, we shall see. Meanwhile, I have work to do. Come, Tirzah." Her mother turned toward the bundles waiting to be undone.

Late in the afternoon Ram returned. He sat by himself, silent, his mouth set in a tight line. Tirzah ignored him. If Ram listened to their uncle Shobal, then he deserved to suffer, and their prig of a cousin Jonathan, too. They'll both be sorry once we get to Canaan, she thought.

Without warning, the terrifying sound of the ram's horn blew shrilly in sharp echoes all over the camp. Tirzah startled, turned to stare to the north. Runners were racing toward them. Breathlessly they shouted the news, "The Egyptians are coming, the Egyptians are coming. The scouts have seen them to the north—chariots, warriors, the Pharaoh, too. Quickly, flee."

Without thinking, Tirzah ran to the tent and began pulling it down. Beside her, Jerioth's strong hands undid the stakes, and together they threw ties and all into the bundle. All over the camp people were wailing or shouting orders, hurrying madly. "What will we do, Jeraheel? Where will we hide?" Her mother's hand reached tremblingly for his arm.

"Stay with the children, Leah, and pray," he answered quickly. "We are still ahead of them. I must go and see what Moses says. We will do what he directs." In a moment Jeraheel was gone.

"It is Shobal you should listen to," Ram shouted after him. Her father did not stop.

Tirzah whirled to face Ram as he spit out his words. "None of this would have happened if we had gone straight on the path to Canaan from the beginning. Now there is no escape but this one." From his belt he pulled his long knife, waving it in the air above his head. "We'll fight to the death," he shouted. "They're not going to take us back as slaves, ever." Before anyone could speak to him, he was running toward Shobal's campsite.

"No, Ram, no," her mother screamed. Tirzah put an arm about Leah's shaking shoulders. "Let him go, Mother—he'll go anyway."

Tirzah hurried back to help the twins and Jerioth, who had already saddled the donkey. Oren held onto one of Sorry's long ears, patting her head and speaking gently to her. Again and again Tirzah looked to the north, staring until her eyes ached for any sign of the approaching army. They were not yet in sight.

Silently she prayed, "Yahweh, please don't let them take us back." There was no time to form the lines of march. Bundles thrown together were quickly secured. Tirzah tightened her belt about the bundle on her back. They were ready to go.

Where? thought Tirzah. Where will they go? How could they climb the mountains quickly enough? Would the Egyptians capture them? In her throat a lump rose, hard and hurting. Like Ram, she would rather die than go back to Egypt.

Suddenly the thought of Abihail came to her, and she wanted desperately to find her. All about her, families stood together, waiting. She could not see Abihail's family, nor Shobal's, where she knew Ram must be standing.

Moses stood on the rock once more, his arms raised high above the people. Tirzah waited with her family, close enough to the rock to see and hear. Above them was the cloud of Glory. Where will it lead us? she wondered. Before Moses could speak, a great cry came from the far edges of the crowd, and every face turned toward the north. Tirzah climbed quickly to Sorry's back and stood upright.

The sight was terrifying. Her heart jumped within her. The army of the Pharaoh was coming. It was too far away to make out anything but the great clouds of dust and what flashed within, surely the metal of swords and chariots gleaming as rays of the setting sun struck them.

In anger, a man cried out, "You, Moses! Was it because there were no graves in Egypt that you brought us to the desert to die?"

A woman shouted, "What have you done to us by bringing us out of Egypt? Didn't we say to you in Egypt, 'Leave us alone; let us serve the Egyptians'?"

Others took up her cry: "It would have been better for us

to serve the Egyptians than to die in the desert."

Tirzah half fell from the donkey's back. As she straightened her bundle, she heard her father shout, "Let Moses speak. Silence, let him speak." Other voices joined with his.

Above the crowds the voice of Moses rang out. "The Lord will fight for you. Stand still and watch."

As Moses spoke, the man next to Tirzah lifted his arm and pointed to the sky. Tirzah heard a murmur of astonishment roll over the crowd as one after another looked above them. Overhead the cloud of Glory moved swiftly until it settled behind them. From plain to sky it blotted out the entire passageway and the Egyptian army behind it, as if a great curtain had been shut.

"Do not be afraid. Stand firm and see the deliverance Yahweh will bring to you today." This time Moses' words had the sound of triumph in them, and Tirzah felt a stab of hope run through her.

The man next to her was pointing to where Moses stood outlined against the sky. "Look," he said, "Moses has lifted his rod."

Tirzah strained to see above the heads around her. Holding Sorry's rope firmly, she tried to mount again, but each time she came close to getting up, Sorry jerked away. The rising wind was making the little donkey restless.

This was more than a rise in the wind, Tirzah thought, pulling her mantle across her mouth. The hot, dry, east wind from the desert blew sand everywhere, seeping into her mouth, eyes, and nose.

A sheltering arm went about her shoulders, pulling her close. Squinting her eyes, Tirzah saw her father's face bent above her. "It will be all right, child," he shouted. "This is the hand of Yahweh. Don't be afraid."

Tirzah threw her arms about his waist and clung tightly to him. "What is happening, Father? Why is the wind so high? Where will we flee?"

"Stand firm and see the Lord fight. That is what Moses said, and that is what we must do." His voice was thin in the wind, but Tirzah nodded. "Can you stay with the donkey?" he shouted. "We will march together with the others, but Ram has chosen to go with his uncle Shobal."

Though he was shouting, Tirzah felt the pain in her father's voice. Ram should have been here with his family, helping. She knew she could handle Sorry as well as Ram, and nodded vigorously. "That's my girl." Her father patted her head. "Oren and the twins will bring the sheep, and Molid and I will see to the carts. When the signal is given, we will march." In another minute he was gone, and Tirzah swallowed hard.

Sorry stood with her head low, her long ears flopping down, her eyes mere slits. Carefully, Tirzah lifted one ear and spoke into it. "It will be all right, Sorry. I'm here to take care of you."

The little donkey brayed as if to say humph.

Though the wind still blew, it seemed to Tirzah as if it had changed directions. It no longer pelted her with sand, but she had to brace herself against its force. She could hear its roaring out to sea.

Night had fallen, covering the mountains and the sky. Tirzah almost dozed, leaning against Sorry. Then people were coming to life all about her in the dimness. Hastily a line of march formed.

As Tirzah wiped the grit from Sorry's leathery hide she saw a flash of red hair flying behind the figure running toward them—Abihail. In a moment she was hugging her tightly. "Oh, Abihail, what will we do?" Tirzah cried, all her fears suddenly back.

"Tirzah, it's a miracle, a miracle—the sea is parting! Moses held his rod up, and then the wind began, and now the water is gone. They said it's piling up like walls and the sea floor is showing."

Tirzah stared at Abihail. "The sea floor is showing?" She could hardly believe her ears.

"Yes, yes," Abihail insisted. "And people are already starting to cross it. I can't stay even a minute more. Look for me later," she shouted back. Stunned, Tirzah watched her disappear into the crowd. Before she could think, the news came, passing from clan to clan, family to family. It was true. They were going to cross the sea, walk through it!

Somewhere behind the cloud of Glory was the Egyptian army. From the side toward Israel, the cloud glowed with light that fell on the people and the sea floor. It was like soft moonlight, and in spite of the heavy wind Tirzah could see enough to walk. She urged the little donkey forward.

Beside her Maacah took hold of Tirzah's hand with fingers that felt like ice. "I am so afraid, Tirzah. What if we get into the middle of the sea and the waters come back again? I can't even swim!" she wailed, clutching Tirzah's hand tightly.

Nahalath answered quickly, "Never mind. You will float." They were almost at the edge of the sandy shore, or where the edge once had been. Underfoot the shore had changed to a wet oozing sand that felt cold on bare skin.

Nahalath let out a little cry. "Oh, Maacah, forgive me. If we live to reach the other side, I promise to give you my best blue fringe." A moment later Nahalath suddenly stopped walking and stood like a statue, her robe flapping in the wind.

"I forgive you, Nal, but don't just stand there. Move, or the Egyptians will surely catch us," Maacah pleaded. Nahalath continued standing as if she were turned to stone.

Tirzah pushed Sorry forward into the wet sand, then turned to wait for Nahalath. Something was wrong. Nahalath stood there as if she no longer heard or saw, though Maacah was shaking her sister and pleading with her. Tirzah stepped back and took one of her cousin's cold hands in her own, rubbing it to warm it.

"Look, Nahalath, there isn't any water now. It's almost dry, just a little damp." All about the sea floor were bunches of weeds, boulders, and muddy sea bottom, dark even in the light from the cloud. It was like nothing Tirzah had ever seen, and her own heart beat fast.

"Come on, Nahalath." Tirzah cajoled. "Yahweh is protecting us. See, we can walk safely here. The bottom is firm." She stamped her feet to show Nahalath. People were beginning to pass around them, and Sorry pressed against her impatiently. This time Tirzah stamped her foot in anger. "We can't just stand here. We have to keep up with the others." Nahalath didn't move.

Again Sorry pushed her nose against Tirzah's shoulder as if to nudge her on. "Come on, please, Nahalath," Tirzah pleaded. "Look, you can hold on to Sorry's rope if you want to." Without speaking Nahalath looked at Tirzah. Tears streamed down her cheeks. Gently Tirzah took her cousin's arm and led her toward the donkey.

With one hand holding tight to Sorry, Nahalath allowed herself to be led, first by Tirzah and then by Maacah. Twice Tirzah stopped to help Sorry out of a tangle of seaweed and then around a boulder that stood in the way. Between them, Maacah and Tirzah guided the silent Nahalath, who seemed unable to move on her own. They tried to hurry to keep up with the others around them. It was all Tirzah could do to keep pushing ahead.

6

Escape

Forced to ride in the cart with old Hanna and the little ones, Oren sat squeezed tightly against the wooden rails. Carefully he stretched his feet between two children sound asleep on the floor. Pale light from the cloud illuminated everything about him: marching people, eerie beds of seaweed, strange stone shapes, and once, what seemed to be the hulk of an old boat half-covered with weeds.

One of the cart wheels struck a large rock, bouncing him against the hard wood of the floor. From her corner Hanna groaned. "Ee, eeh, if the Egyptians do not get us this donkey cart will." Oren watched her old head nod till she fell asleep again.

How can this thing be? he thought. We are in the middle of the sea where the water should be, and it is like dry land.

He yearned to walk, to look closer at the wonders that lay scattered all about him, but his father had sternly forbidden him to leave the cart. Around his neck the precious pouch hung, its contents safe. He would write about this night once they were across the sea and out of danger. Paser's gift of ink and papyrus would not go unused. At the thought of Paser, heaviness crept upon Oren until he felt his eyes closing.

Ram walked behind his uncle Shobal's goats, a silent Abishur at his side. Dreams were like this, he thought. Maybe this was a dream. One minute he stood with the men ready to fight, waiting for the sure death that drove toward them in iron chariots; the next he was running to the sea and finding it indeed gone. Gingerly, he stepped over a strange, quill-like mound that quivered slightly as he looked at it. Was he dreaming? He looked at Abishur as if for an answer.

Abishur's face was full of anguish. "My father was wrong, Ram. I knew it, and I didn't warn you. I should have tried." Anger choked his voice. "He's stubborn as a donkey. No one can make him listen to reason once his mind is made up."

Ram knew it was true. Hadn't he done the same? "Abishur, it isn't like you think. From the start I doubted Moses, doubted Yahweh." Ram pressed a fist tightly to his forehead. "None of this seems real yet."

Abishur shook his head. "There's nothing I can do. Shobal is my father. I'm his son and have to stay with him. What scares me, Ram, is the way he can persuade others to follow him." For a long while the two walked in silence, each wrapped in his own misery.

Cut off from the rest of the family, Tirzah and her cousins plodded on. Tirzah could barely feel her legs, and her arms were heavy weights. Sorry balked at a dark patch of weeds in her path, making Tirzah stumble over her own feet as she reached out to prod her.

Jerking the rope around the donkey's neck, she pulled her to the right. For a while the seabed had been smooth, but now reeds seemed to spread in their way almost everywhere. Suddenly the reason flashed like a light through her—they must be nearing the other shore.

"The shore, the shore," she cried. It was true. Helping hands reached out to grab Sorry's rope, and then her father's strong arms were lifting her, carrying her. Sobbing,

Nahalath fell into her mother's embrace, followed by a tired Maacah. Tirzah closed her eyes, content to be carried like a baby.

She must have slept. Surrounded by piles of baggage, she sat up, brushing the sleep from her eyes. Would she never learn to stay awake? What was all the noise? Cries and shouts of people and the wailing of children, brought her to her feet at once. "The Egyptians must be coming after us!" she exclaimed. Wildly Tirzah looked for her mother and the others. Had they gone without her?

On the rocks behind her, people were standing in thick knots. On the sandy shore below them, others waved their hands, shouting, while some ran back onto the sea floor to hurry the last of the marchers. In the light of the cloud Tirzah saw the whole scene, and her heart beat faster.

The chariots of the Pharaoh were coming. Already they were halfway across the sea floor. Someone screamed as Tirzah ran for the nearest rock, slipping and clawing her way to its top.

"O Yahweh, help us," she cried in her heart. Standing on the rock, she could see the chariots of iron far out in the sea. Every Hebrew man, woman, child, and animal was on shore now, but it was too late to flee farther. Where could they go to hide from such a great army? As if she were bound to the rock, Tirzah stood upon it, unable to take her eyes away from the awful sight before her.

Over the clamor of people wailing and crying to Yahweh, she thought she could hear the shouts of the soldiers. Some of the heavy chariots were bogging down in the mud and getting stuck, causing others following to crash into each other. It was happening everywhere that Tirzah looked. Chariot after chariot turned over, their giant wheels spinning helplessly. From the front line to as far back as she could make out, the chariots were in a tangled mass of accidents.

As she watched, the confusion seemed to grow worse. Some of the chariots now righted were turning back, away from the shore. Tirzah clapped her hands for joy. The Egyptians were retreating.

Then to her horror a path opened, and through it came other chariots driving swiftly, the horses almost flying. Stunned, Tirzah barely noticed the pale light of dawn beginning to streak the sky. All about her people wept and cried out. Then suddenly there was a growing hush.

The wind had changed. From far out in the sea, she heard the sound of thunder roar. The Egyptians had heard it too and were struggling to go back. Too late they saw the sea rushing toward them. In moments their cries were smothered in the swiftly moving water.

Tirzah could hardly believe her eyes. In the light of the morning sun now climbing into the sky, the sea returned to its bed, claiming all in its path. "Drowned," Tirzah whispered. Iron chariots, horses, soldiers, all were gone. The army of Egypt had vanished.

Out of the hushed crowd, Moses' voice rose in a mighty shout of victory. As if on signal, the people echoed him with shout after shout. Tirzah scrambled down the face of her rock and into the crowd.

Everywhere people were singing and dancing and laughing all at once. Almost instantly she was caught up in the nearest group of dancers. A score of tambourines appeared to join the flutes already playing. Never, never had there been such a celebration.

When the sun was at its height, people rested on cloaks and cloths spread on the ground. Those who had food shared it with those who had none. As they ate and rested, a few hardy ones continued to play the pipes. Tirzah stretched herself full length beside Abihail and listened. Overhead a seabird whirled, then glided on its silver-white wings.

"When we get to Canaan," Abihail was saying, "I will ask Mother to make me a tambourine from the scraps of the next goatskin, and you must ask yours to make you one."

Lazily, Tirzah wiggled her toes and pictured herself dancing, tambourine in hand. Secretly, she would much rather have played a pipe like Abishur's. "Listen," Tirzah said half rising on her elbows. Someone was calling for silence. Moses was going to speak, and the word spread throughout the camp like a ripple across a lake.

Once more Moses stood on a rock near the water and raised his arms. In a strong, deep voice he taught them a song of praise to Yahweh for his deliverance. Line after line, the people sang like a great festival chorus:

> I will sing to the Lord,
> > for he is highly exalted.
> The horse and its rider
> > he has hurled into the sea.

It was a mighty song, and Tirzah thought her heart would burst for pride and joy. When it was finished, the people cheered. Surely the Lord *had* risen up in triumph.

"Look." Abihail pointed to the tall woman in the blue robe who stood below Moses on the rock formation, a tambourine held high above her head. "It's Miriam, and she's calling for the women to join her. Oh, Tirzah, how I wish we had our tambourines now," Abihail cried out.

It was true. Women were streaming towards Miriam, shaking their tambourines joyously. The girls watched Miriam join the women and begin the song:

> Sing to the Lord,
> > for he is highly exalted.
> The horse and rider
> > he has hurled into the sea.

58

This time the music was even livelier as the women danced, shaking their tambourines and singing.

It was late in the night when Tirzah lay down by the dying fire. The camp was quiet now, the stars bright overhead. From the north a soft light shone from the cloud. Tirzah sighed a happy little sigh. What a glorious day! She would remember it for the rest of her life.

Oren whistled contentedly, and she glanced over at him sleepily. He shifted his head to look at her. "You know, Tiz, when we get to Canaan, I'm going to write this all down."

Tizrah thought she heard him humming, but her eyes were closing.

7

Forgiven

After the singing and the dancing, Ram found himself walking away from the camp toward its outskirts. He didn't want to be with his uncle Shobal, and he couldn't go back to his father's tent now. Faintly aware that he was heading east, he walked past the last tent. Far enough from the campsite to be alone, he stopped. For a while he sat on the ground, then stretched himself full length and shut his eyes against the soft light of the cloud. The hard ground felt warm and its firmness supporting to his tired body.

How long he lay, if he slept or not, Ram didn't know, but suddenly he was wide awake. A man was standing over him, and instantly Ram knew it was his father. He sat up quickly, but could say nothing.

Kneeling beside him, Jeraheel laid his staff on the ground. "Son, I searched high and low for you everywhere." Impulsively he reached out to grip Ram's shoulder. The pressure of his strong fingers felt good to Ram, though he didn't speak. "When I couldn't find you, I thought—I don't know what."

"How did you find me?" Ram asked, looking away from his father's face.

Jeraheel sat back on his heels, a half-smile on his lips. "You're my son, Ram. I knew you would want to be alone. So when I couldn't find you in the camp, I began thinking of myself in your sandals. They led me here."

Ram covered his face with his hands, unable to hold back the tears. "I doubted Moses, even Yahweh. I thought you were wrong. Uncle Shobal seemed so certain, and it was all so unreasonable to walk into a trap."

Ram couldn't stop the words that came pouring out of him. "I never thought until today, tonight, about the miracles back in Egypt. Why weren't they enough proof for me that Yahweh would really deliver us in his own way, through Moses? Now I know."

Ram looked at his father with anguished eyes. "What's wrong with me, Father? What will I do now?"

Jeraheel put his arm about Ram and pulled him close. "What is wrong with you, Son, is your youth. You are not so long out of childhood, not so long in manhood. What will you do? What all of us must do at times. You will ask forgiveness of Moses and Aaron, then we will go on together to the Promised Land. Maybe we will both be wiser, more thankful now."

Jeraheel ruffled his son's thick, black hair. "You have learned something, eh? Trust in Yahweh is just that, no matter what things look like." Ram looked at his father with new wonder and respect.

As they walked together, Ram's heart beat faster and his mind raced. Ahead of them was the tent of Moses. What would this prophet of Yahweh do to him?

By the tent door a figure sat playing softly on a flute. When Ram and his father drew close, he looked up. "What can I do for you?" Moses asked in a voice both quiet and questioning. "Please sit down," he added, gesturing to a place near the fire.

When they were seated, Jeraheel began. "Moses, this is

my son Ram, who has something to say to you."

Moses, laying his flute on the ground, smiled and said, "Well then, lad, speak."

Nervously, Ram cleared his throat, trying to find the words he knew he must say. "Sir, I have wronged you. I doubted your words. I sided with the men who wanted to go by the direct route to Canaan. I thought you were mistaken about Yahweh's leading, and that he might even let the cloud lead us in the wrong way as a punishment. I—I was wrong. I cannot doubt now that Yahweh is with you." Ram stopped, his cheeks burning hot.

"Ram, I want to tell you something," Moses said gently. "When Yahweh first called me to return to Egypt, I doubted. Was I not still known in Egypt as a deserter? Who would believe me, an old man? I even argued with him and angered him. It's a long story, but in his kindness and patience with me, Yahweh sent my brother Aaron to help me. So you see, you are not the first one to fall into that trap."

Moses gently touched Ram's chin, lifting the boy's face to look up. "From now on, know that Yahweh is with his people to bring them into a good land, the Promised Land. Be brave, lad; keep up your courage. Be strong for your people and faithful to Yahweh."

In Moses' eyes, Ram saw a strength that he would never forget. A sob choked his throat so that he couldn't speak.

"My son and I are grateful. May Yahweh bless you," Jeraheel said, rising to his feet. Ram stood also.

Moses raised his arm in blessing. "May he bless you and keep you." The warmth of the words wrapped themselves around Ram like a wool cloak against the night air. At his father's side, he walked toward their tent with steps lighter than they had been for weeks—or was it his heart?

"Father, if only we could help Abishur. He never doubted Moses. He tried to tell his father, but Uncle Shobal was angry with him and wouldn't listen. Abishur is a faithful son, not like me." Ram bit his lip.

Jeraheel gripped Ram's arm. "Don't look back, Son. Forgiveness washes away the old, lets the new breathe and grow. You are my beloved son, and what you will be in future by the grace of Yahweh will make me proud."

His father patted his arm. "As for Abishur, Yahweh sees his heart. When he is of age to leave his father's tent and take a wife, then we shall see a new Abishur." Ram was thinking of the new Abishur when they entered the tent.

8

Merrie

Tirzah woke to the sound of Ram's whistling. He was hard at work repairing a fishing net, a good sign. In the shade of the tent, her mother sat weaving, a smile playing about her lips. So, Ram was really back to stay. One thing less to worry about, Tirzah thought, drinking in the morning air with its sharp, clean smell of sea. She felt ready for anything this glorious day could hold.

Three hours later, Tirzah sat back on her heels and wiped the sweat from her face. In front of her was a small bundle of sticks. Abihail threw down her own bundle and sat next to it, her cheeks as red as her flaming hair.

"There isn't a stick more to be had," Abihail said. "I think we are lucky to find this much." She tossed her braid back with one hand and brushed away an ant with the other.

Tirzah nodded, but added, "I'd rather pick up a thousand sticks than dry dung any day."

"But you know that's what we have to do next," Abihail retorted.

"The twins went fishing with the men, just because they're boys," Tirzah added. "I'd rather fish any day." As she talked she held the sticks together and twisted a vine about the bundle.

"Not me. I don't ever want to set foot in that sea again. Think of all those dead bodies and chariot wrecks." Abihail shivered. Terrible things had been brought up in the nets along with the fish. "Even this morning, Abishur found a sandal floating near the shore."

It was eerie to think of the dead Egyptians and their horses, trapped under the sea. "At least we know they won't be coming for us ever again," Tirzah said. "And when we get to our own land, I'm never going to leave it." Absently she turned over a rock, uncovering a small lizard. Confused, it lifted its head, then darted away to safety.

Abihail undid her braid and redid its thick shining strands of red-gold. "You know, if all those years ago Joseph hadn't left Canaan and gone down to Egypt in the first place, we wouldn't have to be making this journey back there," she said in a lightly irritated tone of voice.

"But," Tirzah protested, "Joseph didn't go to Egypt on his own, remember. His brothers sold him to the slave traders." For the first time it dawned on her that her great ancestor Joseph had once been a slave, too. Astonished, she stared at Abihail. "No wonder Joseph wanted his bones carried back to Canaan," she said.

Abihail looked puzzled. "What are you talking about?"

To Tirzah it seemed simple. "Look," she said, "Joseph went into Egypt as a slave, and Yahweh made him a great ruler. But he must have wanted to go back to Canaan as a free man. In a way it's like he is going back now and taking us all with him. I mean, all his children and their children's children."

"Enough," Abihail interrupted. "Don't be a donkey. It's we who are carrying that box of old bones back to Canaan."

"You have no imagination," Tirzah said.

"Anyway," Abihail continued, "we still have to cross the

desert, and that's scary. My mother is fretting, but Father says not to worry. Moses knows the desert because he lived in it after he fled Egypt the first time." Raising her head, she threw the finished braid over her shoulder. "Did you know that Moses killed an Egyptian and had to flee Egypt then?"

Tirzah nodded. "I know. Don't forget he did it to save a Hebrew slave's life." Dreamily, she gazed at the distant hills. "I wonder what Canaan will be like? I don't care if we do have to cross the desert to get there. I can't wait to see the Promised Land, can you?"

"No, only I get the shivers when I think of the desert and meeting up with wild Bedouin who think they own it all," Abihail said. "Who'd want their desert anyway? Not me."

"Nor me," Tirzah added. She could think of a hundred tales about the terrors of the desert. Bare ground baked in the sun's heat stretched endlessly. Huge barren rocks rose out of the sand to loom over the empty wastes. Giant buzzards flew above white, bleached skulls. She shuddered. People died in the desert for lack of water. Suddenly Tirzah's throat felt dry. "We'd better get these sticks back to camp," she said, jumping to her feet.

In the days that followed, the camp began to feel like home. For a moment Tirzah was shocked when the cry came ringing from tent to tent: "The cloud is moving. Prepare to march."

Tirzah looked inquiringly at her father. "To the desert, Father?"

"Yes, straight into the Desert of Shur," he answered. "We have had enough rest to fatten us all for the journey. Just look at your mother."

Tirzah smiled as her mother pretended an angry frown. She could no longer hide signs of the coming baby in spite of her loose robe. It was true, though. All of them looked healthy. There was a new sparkle in her father's eyes and a strength in his stride. Even Oren's face was ruddy.

When the march began, Jeraheel took Sorry with him. Freed from supervising the donkey, Tirzah walked easily. Her legs seemed to have grown new strength and didn't tire so easily. She was glad to have her strong sandals. No one could make sandals like her uncle Onan, his back bent from years of hunching over his work. The pair he had crafted for her were of sturdy leather, a gift on her birthday.

By midday all the old aches were back, and Tirzah was sure she could not take another step. Her sandals no longer kept the hot gritty dust from her tender feet. By the time the signal was given to stop, her feet were all she could think of.

They rested under makeshift shelters set on poles, and Tirzah kicked off her sandals. The men and older boys went off to their own gathering place. The twins, lean and brown, their black curly hair more tangled than ever, were sitting with Oren a few yards away. Their heads were bent together over something.

Tirzah closed her eyes and tried not to think that the march would soon begin again. She could not bear to put her feet back into her sandals, but she couldn't go barefoot either.

"Here take these." Oren stood before her impatiently thrusting two squares of sheepskin towards her. "Hurry up and take them. They're for your feet. See, Benj has put thongs at the sides." Oren pushed the skins into her hands, and Tirzah saw that he was already wearing a similar pair on his feet. They were laced about his legs a few inches above his ankles.

She took the skins, looking at them curiously. "Do you think they will work?" she asked.

Before Oren could answer, she was already tying them on. Her sandals fit snugly round the wraps, and the softness of the wool cushioned her feet. "They work well," she called to Benj, who looked up at her and grinned. She knew it was Benj and not Reuben by the fresh cut an ill-tempered goat had given him on the right cheek.

Jerioth too was wearing a pair and carrying skins to her mother. Tirzah laughed at the way all of them looked, but it was a great idea. For the rest of the afternoon she wore her boots. She was surprised that though she was sweating everywhere, the boots seemed to help keep out the heat and absorb the sweat.

When they stopped to camp for the night, the air was already cooling. Tirzah stood waiting for her turn at the water skin, wishing it were a well instead of a bag of water. "This water must do us tomorrow, too," Jerioth cautioned.

The desert stretched for miles beyond them without a palm or a spring in sight. Tirzah let her ration slide around in her mouth before she swallowed it. She would have liked more, but even the animals must have their share. Sorry complained loudly at the small allotment Tirzah gave the tired little donkey.

Still thirsty, Tirzah took a fig from the dish her mother was sending to old Hanna. She walked slowly towards the part of camp where Hanna's tent was, savoring the sweetness of the fig on her tongue. Up ahead her uncle Shobal sat by his campfire, talking to a group of men. What was he up to now?

"Hi! Going somewhere?" Tirzah spun around to face her cousin Jonathan. He was taller than his brother Abishur, and in a way better looking. His arms rippled with strength, and the strands of hair that curled about his forehead were thick and dark.

Still, there was something about him that she didn't like. He was not a good loser, sulking when he lost a race or game.

She greeted him politely. "I'm on my way to old Hanna with a bit of fruit. Sometimes she forgets to eat at all."

"So, one good deed deserves another. I'll walk with you and keep you company, eh?" Jonathan smiled, a smile that was part of the charm he had when he wasn't sulking.

Tirzah turned toward Hanna's campsite. "Why not?" she said. "One is free in the desert."

Jonathan laughed. "Free in the desert? Not yet, Cousin, not yet. But when we get to Canaan, then we shall see how free peoples live. By the way, I haven't seen Ram around for a while. Is he okay?"

Tirzah pursed her lips. So that was why Jonathan wanted to walk with her—to ask about Ram. Innocently, she looked up at him. "He's fine, couldn't be better." She would tell him nothing.

"I gather that Uncle Jeraheel is a bit put out by Ram and the rest of us who don't go along blindly with everything this Moses and Aaron have to say." He waited for Tirzah to catch up. "But I don't expect you to bother your pretty head about all that."

His smug tone was too much to bear. "I'll tell you what I think," Tirzah heard herself saying. "I think you just can't take losing. Moses was right. Didn't we cross the sea, and didn't Pharaoh's army drown?" Tirzah walked quickly, not waiting for an answer. "Or maybe you didn't cross, and I'm just talking to a ghost."

"I know a miracle when I see one," Jonathan answered quickly, his long strides easily keeping up with her short swift ones. "But did it ever occur to you that Yahweh might have saved his people by a miracle in spite of their foolishness? Doesn't it stand to reason that if we'd marched straight to Canaan right from the start, we'd be safe in our own land all the sooner?"

He stopped walking. "Slow down a minute. I'm not the enemy, Tirzah. All we want is to see our people safe in a place they can call their own. We follow Yahweh, but not blindly. Does Yahweh plow the land for a man, or hunt down his food? Doesn't he expect us to use our heads? Moses is a good man, but he is old, Tirzah. We're talking about taking care of thousands of people, many of them children."

Tirzah had no answer. Jonathan wasn't the enemy, and what he said seemed right. But if Moses was wrong, why did Yahweh listen to him? She glanced at Jonathan's earnest face and softened. "Sorry, Jonathan. Anyway, we're on the way to Canaan, and Pharaoh and his army are gone. It can only be better from here on."

"That's just what some of us are trying to see to, and it's why we've got to use our heads," Jonathan insisted. Tirzah quickened her steps, and they walked the rest of the way to Hanna's campsite in silence.

Hanna wasn't alone. As they entered the tent, a slender girl turned to face them—Merrie, Paser's niece. Tirzah was so surprised to see the Egyptian girl that for a moment she stared at her, then managed to stammer, "Merrie, I didn't know you had come."

A shadow flitted across the girl's plain, almost-square face. "When my uncle died on the night of the great judgment, I fled to the house of Peleg, the Hebrew. Peleg often brought my uncle a certain plant he required for his inks. I had no family left. I knew that your God was stronger than the gods of Egypt, so I begged to go with Peleg's household as a servant."

Hanna interrupted in her thin voice. "She is a good girl. I am glad to have her. Peleg owed me, and I took Merrie in exchange. Now what brings you two here?"

As Tirzah explained, Merrie offered two small honeycakes to Jonathan, who ignored the girl as if she did not exist. With lowered eyes and trembling lips, Merrie turned to Tirzah, the plate still before her. Carefully, Tirzah lifted one of the little cakes. "Thank you, Merrie. I will take it back to Oren."

A small light of pleasure shone from Merrie's dark, fawnlike eyes. "My uncle was fond of your brother." Quickly, she bowed her head and withdrew to a corner of the tent.

Outside the tent, Tirzah kept an icy silence while Jonathan raved on and on. "Viper. A good girl? The only good Egyptian is a dead one. Her kind ought to be left to die in the desert. Fond of the boy—fond of slaves, was he? Maybe old Hanna can take having an Egyptian slave, but the sight of an Egyptian makes me sick." He turned his head and spit the way Tirzah had seen the men do to show their anger.

"She had better not get in my way," Jonathan said. Still in his ugly mood as he left her on the path to her tent, he grumbled a farewell.

Tirzah walked on, alone with the night sounds of the camp—a crying child, and here and there snatches of voices. A strange thought about Merrie puzzled her. What if she, Tirzah, had been born an Egyptian? What if she were Merrie and Merrie were the Hebrew daughter? How many like Jonathan would spit at the sight of her? Poor Merrie. Tirzah hurried inside the tent.

9

Meat from the Sky

Better? Tirzah licked her dry lips. Had she said that things could only get better? After three days of marching, there was still no water to be found. Not a trickle, not a mud puddle, nothing. The land they walked on now was hard and dry, littered with rocks. Here and there small clumps of tough wilderness grass provided food for the goats and sheep, but for people there was nothing.

Maacah mopped her streaming face for the dozenth time. "Oh, look, Tirzah, look over there—buzzards." She pointed to the east where a small flock of great dark buzzards soared slowly in the sky. "They know we're here," she said, "and they're just waiting for one of the animals to die of thirst."

Tirzah shaded her eyes and looked at the birds. Wicked things, she thought. Where did they get their water from out here? Or did they live on the creatures who died in the desert? Horrible thought. When the march stopped at last, she forgot everything but water.

At every campsite children cried, some demandingly, some softly. It was hot, and what little rations of water were left satisfied no one. Not far away Moses and Aaron were trying to talk to a gathering crowd of people. Angry voices protested. "Do you expect us to cross this desert without water?" one demanded. "Just what are we to drink?"

Near enough for Tirzah to hear him, Moses answered. "Tomorrow we will reach a place where there is water. Be strong just a little while longer." Tomorrow, thought Tirzah, seemed so far away. How could she sleep tonight? How could anyone sleep? She might have guessed that if anyone could, she could. Already the line of march was forming when she woke.

In the afternoon they came to water. Soon, soon she would drink as much as she could hold. The thought was lovely, but a sudden wailing noise from those nearest the water startled her. "Bitter, the water is bitter. It's not fit to drink." Tirzah wanted to wail, too.

Someone called out, "Moses, this is your fault. What are we going to do now?" Other voices joined in with angry words. Tirzah thought she would wail. Why was this happening? She knew she was going to die of thirst. In her misery she barely heard the words of Moses as he cried out to Yahweh.

Next to her, Maacah pushed against the man in front of them. "What's he doing? I can't see," Maacah complained. "Are they drinking the bitter water?"

The tall man in front of them was impatient. "Hush, hush. Wait a minute. Moses is throwing a branch into the water. Now he's scooping up water and drinking it! Yes, he's drinking it."

From the front lines came shouts of wild joy. "It's sweet, the water is sweet." Others took up the cry, "A miracle, a miracle, the water is good."

Under the starry night, her stomach full, the warm campfire dancing lazily in little yellow flames, Tirzah sighed happily.

Between them, Jerioth and Leah had cooked a good meal

from their little store of dried corn and fruit. Tirzah looked at her mother leaning against her father's shoulder contentedly. Jerioth's family had already gone to their own tent.

Tirzah was glad her mother didn't mind her sleeping outside with Oren and Ram. It was so lovely under the stars. Her eyes found the cloud hovering over the camp. At night it glowed like a night-fire, as if angels camped in the sky to watch over them.

Yahweh had spoken to Moses this very day. Tirzah thought of Yahweh's great promise passed from tribe to tribe. If the people would listen carefully to Yahweh's words and do them, he would not bring on them any of the sickness he had sent on the Egyptians. How great Yahweh is, she thought, and fell instantly asleep.

When the march stopped again it was at Elim, a green oasis in the desert. Lush palms grew everywhere, and there were plenty of springs of fresh water. Tirzah patted Sorry's gaunt, bony side as the animal drank her fill.

"You'll have plenty to eat today, and when we come to the Promised Land, I will make your coat shine once more," she whispered. Sorry paid no attention to anything but the business at hand—slurping the water before her.

Maybe the little donkey knew, Tirzah thought, that tomorrow or the next day the march would start again, and the water would disappear again.

And so it had. Only this time more than the water had disappeared after the march from Elim into the Desert of Sin. The small evening meal, a handful of raisins and goat curd, left even Tirzah hungry. She glanced at Ram sitting cross-legged near the campfire, listening to Jonathan seated next to him. Ram no longer went to their uncle Shobal's tent, but Jonathan still brought news of the camp each night.

Tirzah listened, half-admiring Jonathan's strong young face as the firelight shone on it, and half-irritated by his words. "The whole camp is rumbling with unrest. From tribe to tribe the plea is the same—bread and meat. It cannot go on much longer this way, I tell you, or the people will rebel."

Jonathan spat on the ground and continued. "The leaders are saying we might as well have stayed in Egypt. Better to have done that than to starve to death in the desert. For two months and fifteen days we've followed this Moses." Jonathan paused, but Ram said nothing.

Tirzah's arms shivered in the cool night air, and she moved closer to the fire. What if Jonathan was right after all? What if the people had already disobeyed Yahweh, and now he would let them die in the desert?

Someone was coming up the path, singing softly in the dark—Jerioth. Her voice was clear, high, and sweet. The words of the song fell and rose like gentle doves in flight:

I will sing to the Lord,
    for he is highly exalted.
The horse and its rider
    he has hurled into the sea.

Tirzah listened carefully, remembering how the words of the song went:

In your unfailing love you will lead
    the people you have redeemed.
In your strength you will guide them. . . .

Tirzah shut her eyes and then opened them quickly to look toward the cloud of soft fire above the camp. It was still there. Did Yahweh see their hunger? Had he forgotten how little food there was?

Maybe Yahweh didn't worry about such things. She wished she knew. She wasn't going to like it much if this was the way things were to be all the way to the promised land.

The thought of meat roasting on a spit, its fat dripping into the fire, made her mouth water. In a moment the vision was gone, leaving her staring at the low flames of the dying fire.

Morning came and with it the sound of the ram's horn calling the people before Moses and Aaron. Oren, limping more than usual, leaned on his crutch, his face drawn with pain. Tirzah felt a knot tighten in her stomach. Oren was the weaker one in the family. Without the right food, what would happen to him? With the question still in her mind, she turned to her father and caught him looking sadly at Oren limping ahead of them. With a loud whoop, he scooped up the boy, crutch and all, pretending a game as he ran with him toward the meeting rock.

Those closest to the rock heard the words that Aaron spoke clearly, while those further away received them as the message was relayed from tribe to tribe, clan to clan. Tirzah stood with Maacah, Nahalath, and Rachel by the women of her family. She was near enough to see the prophet and his brother standing above them on the great rock.

Even as Aaron's voice rang out, a strange, wonderful thing happened. The cloud above the camp began to shine brighter than it had ever shone before in daylight. "The glory of the Lord," Aaron shouted as the people lifted their eyes to the shining cloud.

Yahweh had promised them meat by this very twilight and bread in the morning. Afterwards, Tirzah listened as her mother explained again what they were to do.

"Tomorrow you and Oren will go out with the others and gather the bread. You must each gather five omers, as Moses commanded. An omer for each person." Leah paused to catch her breath. "No more and no less, please. To help you, I have marked a line on the baskets." She held a basket before Tirzah, pointing to the small dark line below its edge.

Straightening her back, Leah sighed. "Ooch, my back is not willing to bend so long anymore." Tirzah smiled at her mother, heavy with the coming baby, and thought how beautiful her face was with its smooth skin, smiling mouth, and small turned-up nose. If it was a girl, maybe this one would look like her mother. Tirzah's nose was long and straight like her father's and Ram's and Oren's.

She was startled from her thoughts by shouts and cries from runners coming into the camp. "Get your sticks quickly. Quail, the quail are landing. Hurry, the air is black with them." Tirzah looked to the southwest, where the sky had suddenly grown dark with a low, living cloud of birds—the quail. Weary from their long flight, there was no escape.

The birds were small and a lot of work to clean, but their meat was delicious. Jerioth laughed as Oren blew a small feather, wafting it from hand to hand. "These feathers will make a soft pillow for the new little one," she said, sorting through for the tiny under-feathers. Oren sneezed, sending her pile flying, Jerioth scurrying, and the rest of them laughing.

"May I join the fun?" It was Abishur.

"If you have brought your flute, then you may join us," Tirzah's mother teased lightly.

From inside his tunic, Abishur withdrew the flute and held it high. "Will this old thing do?" he asked, and grinned. The flute was unlike any other Tirzah had ever seen, its smooth wood carved with tiny vines and leaves.

"Old thing, is it?" Oren said. "Then just let me throw it in the fire for you. You can have the one Peleg traded me for an Egyptian armband I found by the sea."

As Oren reached for the flute, Abishur laughed and swung it out of harm's way. "Sorry. I've promised to defend the old thing," he said. "But fetch yours, Oren, and perhaps the two will become friends."

Tirzah smiled. How different Abishur was from his brother Jonathan. The firelight played on Abishur's bowed head, the color of ripe wheat. But that wasn't the only difference between the two. Broad-shouldered though he was, Abishur had none of Jonathan's quick temper.

If he had been the older brother, Tirzah thought, he might have been more like his father, Shobal, and less like his gentle mother, Rebekah. The idea that there could be two of her uncle Shobal struck her as funny. Even Jonathan was not that bad.

The men were returning. Her father's voice was lighter than she had heard it lately. "Molid, come sit, and we shall see how these young men play. Tirzah, fetch your mother's tambourine. If I am going to sing, I want a lot of help." Tirzah ran to the tent.

Song after song they sang until at last Abishur laid his flute aside and rose to go. The embers of the fire glowed in the stillness. There was a contented quiet, full of their recent music. It had been a perfect night, except that Abihail had missed it. Tirzah knew how it irritated Abihail to miss an opportunity to be near Abishur. Oh, well, she couldn't help it if Abishur came so often to see them. He was a cousin, wasn't he?

10

Old Hanna's Child

In the morning sun the desert floor sparkled with what looked like white frost. Everywhere near the tamarisk trees, women and children where picking up the thin white flakes. Tirzah sat on her heels and carefully lifted a flake. It lay in her hand as light as a feather and cool to her touch. So this is the bread Moses meant, she thought. It was unlike anything she had ever seen. Gently she began to gather the tiny wafers into her basket.

She was finished before Oren and started back to the tent. Ephan, the only child of Hameel, the cartmaker, joined her. Glad for the company, Tirzah waited for her.

Ephan was broadly built like her father, her hands large and strong. Tirzah knew that the girl worked like a son with her father, helping him fashion the heavy cart wheels. She was a cheerful girl, though she seldom had time for anything but work. Tirzah liked her and secretly admired Ephan's strength.

Ephan carried two large baskets holding as much as Tirzah's and Oren's together. Since there were only three in Ephan's family, Tirzah was curious. Moses' instructions were to gather an omer for each person, no more, no less. She couldn't help asking, "Ephan, are you gathering bread for another household?"

Ephan shook her head. "No, no. Father's order this morning was to gather enough for two days because tomorrow I will be needed to help him fix an axle for Shobal's cart. You know that we are a large family, though we are but three." She laughed at her joke and went on. "So, I thought I had better take enough to satisfy our appetites for both days."

Tirzah wondered if Ephan's reasons would satisfy Moses. "Oh, well, I suppose in your case it's all right to gather for two days." As she said the words, a little twinge of guilt pinched her inside. She ignored it and went on chatting with Ephan about the coming day's small events.

As soon as the morning sun had turned hot, the white flakes of manna vanished like the morning dew, leaving no trace on the ground. Tirzah's supply of manna, as it was called, baked into a delicious bread with the faint taste of honey. She was sorry when the last of it disappeared into Ram's mouth. They were full now, but what about tomorrow?

"Come, Tirzah, and help me clear these bowls away."

Her mother's voice broke into her thoughts, making Tirzah blurt out, "Will there be more tomorrow? Manna, I mean. Do you think it will come again?"

Leah's eyes were surprised. "I never thought of there not being more. Why shouldn't there be more? Didn't Moses say we would have bread to eat? Didn't he say not to leave any of it overnight, not one bit? Why shouldn't it be there tomorrow, and the day after that?"

Her mother picked up a mat and carried it into the tent, letting Tirzah know that the conversation was ended. Tirzah sighed as she lifted a small crumb from her skirt. She hoped her mother was right.

In the morning as soon as the dew lifted from the ground,

Tirzah hurried to look. It was there, white flakes everywhere around the trees and shrubs. Yahweh's gift of bread had come again. With a little dancing step, she set her basket down and began to gather the wafers.

A footstep behind her made her turn to look. Ephan. "But I thought you would not come today. What happened, Ephan?"

Ephan's face was red, her eyes swollen as though she had been crying. "I told Father what Moses said, not to take more than one day's worth. This morning there was no manna left in our jar, nothing but a stinking mass of worms." She screwed up her face at the memory of it.

"Father blames me, though I had nothing to do with it. Now I must hurry and get back to help him before he gets into such a temper as he will never get out of this day."

Ephan bent quickly to her work, and Tirzah went on with hers. She was sorry for the girl who really wasn't to blame for her father's stubborn ways.

Again, when the sun became hot, the manna disappeared. Tirzah wasn't worried. They had enough for today, and tomorrow she would gather more. On the day before the Sabbath, she and Oren brought home a two-days' supply, just as Moses had instructed. This time it didn't go wormy or smell. On the Sabbath morning there was no manna lying on the desert floor. A few people who had counted on it went home with empty baskets.

• • •

A lone hawk hung motionless on the air high above the rocky ledge on which Ram sat. He could have spent this Sabbath in the camp talking lazily with the others, but the wilderness had drawn him like a magnet. Something in him felt the desert's emptiness as if it were a part of him.

Overhead the hawk soared. Like the bird, Ram felt alone.

He had changed. In Egypt he'd been a child, but no more. The hawk was circling, climbing higher as if inspecting the desert below. Shading his eyes, Ram watched the bird search for its food. Its sharp eyes were a wonder, and even at that great height not a creature as small as a mouse would escape its sight. Ram turned away stricken. Why had he been so blind?

He had fallen once into the trap of foolishly following after his uncle Shobal and the others who refused to believe Moses. Closing his eyes, he whispered, "Surely, Yahweh, you showed your might through your servant Moses. Who could doubt your wisdom now?"

But he had doubted. Why was it that one moment his heart was light, knowing his father's love for him was unchanged, and the next wretched, empty, worthless? Would he doubt the next time his faith was tested? Was he destined to be a failure? After a long while, Ram opened his eyes, saw that the hawk was gone, and let himself down from the ledge to the rocks below.

His sandals made little sound as he stepped from rock to rock, watching carefully for the small scorpions that liked to shelter from the heat in the shadow of the boulders. Halfway down he stood still and listened to a muffled sound coming from somewhere close by.

At first Ram thought it was a small animal snuffling, but as he listened he was sure it was a child crying softly. Cautiously, he made his way around a large overhanging rock toward the sounds. Suddenly he stood directly in front of the small huddled figure of a girl, her face streaming with tears.

The fear that leapt into her face startled Ram. "It's all right," he explained quickly. "I didn't know you were here. I'm sorry. Look, if you've hurt yourself, I can go and get help." He felt the awkwardness of his words even as he said them. The girl was obviously not harmed. She was an Egyptian girl, probably one who had fled Egypt as a servant to one of his people.

Hastily, she got to her feet, backing away from him toward the rock wall. "I'm fine now, thanks. It's nothing." She brushed the wetness from her face, then looked up at him, her chin set defiantly, much like Tirzah's, Ram thought.

"Well then, if you are all right, I'm glad. My name is Ram." He stood awkwardly, not sure whether to leave her or not.

The girl bowed her head slightly and replied, "I am Merrie, servant to Hanna, the midwife."

Ram knew that old Hanna no longer practiced her midwifing, though some still called her by that name. "I'm going to the camp that way now," he said. "Shall I walk you back?"

A flush of deep color rose in the girl's cheeks.

"Oh no, no, I must run back quickly. I've been gone too long already." In a single leap she was on the rock below him, scampering like a deer lightly down to the desert floor. Ram watched her half amused, half admiring the girl's quickness. She would be safely back at camp long before he arrived there himself.

Something glittered on the rock and caught Ram's eye as he turned to go. It was a bracelet, small enough to fit a slender arm. The girl's perhaps? He picked it up and examined its finely carved silver closely. He could make little of the markings, though it looked like Egyptian writing. Oren might know. Stuffing the bracelet into the pouch at his belt, he leapt to the next rock. He would have to find her and return the thing. As he reached the ground, he wondered again why she had been crying.

At Hanna's tent, Merrie paused for breath. She had run all the way. This time no young children had pelted her with small stones the way they had yesterday as she bent to draw water for herself and Hanna. She could hear their voices all over again when she thought of it: "Dirty, dirty Egyptian. Go home, go home." The child who had started the chant was a boy of about six or seven. Merrie had hurried away as quickly as she could.

The tent flap was up, and Merrie stepped quietly inside. Old Hanna sat nodding over a half-eaten honeycake. Home, Merrie thought, where is home now? Gently, she removed the cake from the gnarled fingers and laid it nearby. She would go and draw water for them now while others rested. Then she remembered: on the Sabbath all work was forbidden. Tomorrow she would find another way, perhaps in the afternoon when the sun grew too hot even for the children.

It was hot now, and Merrie undid the long black braid of hair that hung to her waist. How often Paser had told her that she was blessed with the most beautiful hair in Egypt. It was true that it grew unusually thick and would wave and curl about if she let it. She shook it out now, smoothing it, then braiding it tightly once more.

Finished, she rubbed her cheeks to erase all tear marks, feeling again the squareness of her face. She was plain, hair or no hair. She had gone to the house of Peleg as she was, dressed in her Egyptian clothes, the same ones she wore now. Thoughtfully, she smoothed the soft linen she was so used to. Maybe she could make herself more like the Hebrew women. Dress like they did so she wouldn't stand out.

Behind her Hanna woke with a little snore, and Merrie knelt at her feet. "What is it, little bird, that makes you look so thoughtful?" Hanna asked, her old eyes awake and sharp. She listened to Merrie's plan, nodding now and then in approval.

When they were done, Merrie turned round and round for Hanna to see. The wool robe was loose and simple. "From top to bottom you look like I did when I was a girl," the old woman said softly.

"Yahweh has been kind to me," Merrie said. "I hope he will not mind that I dress like his people."

Hanna drew the girl to her for a moment then held her at

arm's length. "If you will obey Yahweh's words and listen to them carefully, will he not be pleased with you? You too have fled Egypt and turned away from all the gods of Egypt to Yahweh, and he has brought you safely here."

The old woman paused and placed a thin hand under Merrie's chin. "In all the years I have laid many babies in their mother's arms, not once have I had a child of my own. Do you think Yahweh brings me a child in my old age? One who will be more comfort to me than I can be to her?"

Merrie's eyes brimmed with tears. "I will be a daughter to you as long as Yahweh lends me breath."

Hanna chuckled. "May that be longer by far than what I expect he shall lend me. These old bones have lived a long time. I only hope they will last until we get to the Promised Land."

Anxiously, Merrie watched Hanna make her way slowly and painfully from the tent. She would care for the old woman, see that she rested more and ate well. If only she would not die and leave her here alone. "Please, Yahweh, please do not let her die," she prayed.

11

Hidden Danger

Merrie rubbed a small drop of precious oil across her dry, cracked lips. For days the cloud had led them through terrible land barren of all but jagged hills. There was no water anywhere. She had given the last small portion of water to Hanna the night before. This camp was no better than any of the others had been, nothing but dry, hard ground. When would Yahweh bring them to water? With a sigh, she laid their mats on the tent floor.

While she waited for Hanna to return from a visit to a neighboring woman, Merrie sat under the open tent flap that formed a canopy overhead. She reached for her braid and undid it for the night, bending her head to comb the thick dark tresses. Behind her waterfall of hair, she was unaware of the silent figure that stood watching her.

Ram wanted to say something, let the girl know that he had come, but the sight of the long, dark, silky hair that spilled into her lap like a robe kept him staring. He moved slightly, and in an instant she was on her feet.

"I'm sorry—I didn't mean to startle you," he stammered. "I found this, and I think it's yours."

In his hand was the small carved bracelet. She knew it was hers. With burning cheeks, she took it from him. "I must have lost it the other day. Thank you for bringing it to me."

Puzzled, she looked at him. "How knew you that it was mine?" Her slip of tongue into the formal speech of her ancestors made her cheeks flush hotter.

"Easy. For one thing, I found it where you had been sitting on the rock. And for another, I figured that the carvings were Egyptian." He smiled at her, and she smiled back.

"My uncle Paser gave it to me when I first came to live in his house." She turned the bracelet around, searching for one of the carvings. "There," she said, pointing to what looked to Ram like a crude stick figure standing at an archway. "That one represents me entering my uncle's household."

Ram nodded. "Yes, I see," he said. "Or I think I do," he added. She laughed then, and he grinned. "Well, I'd better be off. I only came to return the bracelet to you." He hadn't meant to say it that way, but the words leapt out before he could stop them. His feet wouldn't obey him either. Awkwardly stumbling over a piece of firewood, he backed away from the tent and bolted off into the night.

Ram was glad for the dark that wrapped itself around the camp. All he could think of was the girl and how transformed she was from the last time he had seen her curled up on a rock crying. When she smiled, she was beautiful. She seemed to him like a vision framed in the loveliest hair he had ever seen. What was it that had made her cry? He wished he know.

With a start, Ram realized he had run past the path to his own tent toward the broad plain glowing faintly in the light from the fiery cloud above it. Here and there rocks rose like dark shadowy figures. Drawn by the empty night, he walked on toward the large outcrop of rock ahead of him.

Someone was playing a lyre. The sound came, not from

the direction of the camp behind him, but from the plain directly in front. Curious, Ram walked toward it. At the edge of the hill of rock he stopped. Not far ahead was the mysterious player, seated on a rock with his back to Ram. As the man began to sing, Ram stood transfixed. It was the voice of Moses.

Softly he sang,

Lord, you have been our dwelling place
throughout all generations.
Before the mountains were born
or you brought forth the earth and the world,
from everlasting to everlasting you are God.

Ram's heart beat quickly. His feet made no sound as he stepped back and turned toward the camp. Behind him the song continued. In the desert night the words felt real to Ram. Yahweh watched over his people here, now.

All at once Ram wanted nothing more than to sleep. Like a tired runner after a good race, he headed home. Most of the tents were dark, their owners asleep. With a frown he looked toward his uncle Shobal's tent, where a freshened fire blazed. In its light sat a group of at least a dozen men. What were they up to this time? Jonathan would report it all to him tomorrow. Tonight Ram did not care.

In the morning the heat rose quickly. Ram led the goats to feed on the sparse thorny stems of a tough desert plant that only they could stomach. Their thin hides clung so that he could see the shape of their knobby bones. A cloud of dust made him look up. It was Jonathan, running in spite of the thick heat. "Ram, come quickly. Some of the flocks have died, and the people are ready to stone Moses." Jonathan stopped, out of breath.

Ram was on his feet instantly, his hand reaching for knife and sling. "We must go to his aid at once." He scooped up a handful of stones and placed them into the pouch at his belt.

Stunned disbelief covered Jonathan's face. "What are you saying, Ram? Don't you know that everyone is in agreement? This man Moses can no longer lead us. If we don't have water, we'll all die. Come on, man, think. We have to act like men here for the sake of the women and children." Jonathan's words were the words Ram had heard before, from his uncle Shobal.

Ram turned quickly toward the camp, calling back as he went, "My father and I will defend him to the death." This time Ram knew as he ran, there was no question in his mind—Moses was Yahweh's servant. How could they get to the Promised Land without him?

In front of Moses and Aaron, the crowd stood listening in sullen silence. Ram saw his uncle Caleb head and shoulders above those standing round him, and pushed his way to him. His uncle waved and made room to let him in.

"Moses and Aaron have called for the elders to walk on ahead with them to the place where God will provide water for the people. Afterward we will all follow," Caleb said in a low voice. "All the same, the mood of the people worries me. A mob like this can quickly turn into an unreasoning beast."

From the corner of his eye, Ram saw a short, thin man drop the fist-size stone he had been holding. Surely they would not stone Moses and Aaron, not while he and his uncle Caleb stood by. "If it should come to a fight, we'll be ready to stand against any who defy Yahweh's chosen," Ram declared.

His uncle looked down, a smile on his broad face. "That's the spirit." Then his face grew serious. "How can they forget so soon the floggings and death that were our lot in Egypt?"

The crowd was beginning to disperse. Putting a great hand on Ram's shoulder, Caleb guided him toward the tents. The air seemed thick with grumbling voices. Caleb kept his low as he spoke. "A free thirsty man is a thousand times better than a thirsty slave, eh, Ram? We have not lost anyone yet to thirst or hunger. These bellyachers make me sick."

Ram nodded, glad for his uncle's heavy pawlike hand on his shoulder. What if his uncle Shobal had led his men to fight against the Egyptian army back at the Red Sea? What if they had died there because they did not wait for Yahweh? The thought was terrible.

By late afternoon Ram was watering the goats at the very place Moses had predicted Yahweh would provide water. One of the young goats nosed between two of his elders and was butted for his trouble. Ram guided him to a spot where he could drink. Tirzah led another youngster to an open place. Theirs were the last of the animals at the watering hole. Above them the water fell in a steady stream from a crevice in the overhanging rock.

Carefully Ram cupped a handful of the water, marveling at its coldness. Nashon, elder of the tribe of Judah, had seen the water rush from the rock when Moses struck it with his rod. Ram brought his hand to his mouth and drank. It left a faintly earthy taste on his tongue.

Tirzah came and knelt by him, letting her hands float just beneath the surface of the water. "It was a miracle, wasn't it?" She raised her head to look at Ram. "It tastes like other water," she said, "but I keep thinking it shouldn't. I wish I could put some in a special jar and save it forever."

Ram tweaked her nose with his wet hand. "Silly, it isn't the water, it's the way Yahweh provided it that's the miracle."

Tirzah dried her wet hands and thought a minute. "I think that the whole thing is a miracle, the water and the rock. The only thing I can't figure out is why Yahweh didn't give us water at each of the campsites." She turned to face her brother. "Why didn't he, Ram? He could have."

For what seemed a long while, Ram didn't answer. In the stillness, Tirzah could almost hear the desert listening. It was getting late, and the goats were beginning to circle restlessly. When he spoke, the words came slowly.

"Yahweh could have, Tiz, but we do have bread, and none of us have died of thirst."

"I still don't understand," Tirzah insisted.

Ram sent a pebble skipping across the water as he answered. "What if we'd tried to do the whole thing alone? I mean, escape from Egypt and cross the desert?"

"But that would be impossible," Tirzah said. "In the first place, nobody could have made Pharaoh let us go."

Ram nodded. "Exactly. And what if Yahweh wanted to make it clear that he was behind the whole thing, that he was leading us?"

Again Tirzah interrupted. "But that is what he did. We have the cloud, and the Egyptian army is gone, all those things. I don't get it."

Ram sighed and tried again. "What I mean is, suppose he had made the whole crossing easy for us, plenty of water and meat every day, what then? We wouldn't even know what he had done for us."

Ram paused, his face clouded with effort. "Look." He picked up a handful of rock and soil and held it in front of her. "This is a wilderness we're crossing, not some lush garden, and Yahweh is the one who will take us through it. We won't ever forget that it was a desert."

Tirzah nodded. "Well, some might forget, but I don't think I would."

A shadow crossed Ram's face, and he said, "How do you know for sure? It's easier than you think, Tiz, to forget to trust Yahweh. I ought to know."

Warmth rushed to Tirzah's cheeks. "But you didn't," she stammered. "I mean, you made a mistake," she finished weakly.

Ram's face reddened. "Remember it, Tiz." He turned to gaze at the hills. "And another thing," he said abruptly, "when trouble comes, that's the time to show your trust. Let's go." Quickly he scooped up his staff and began calling the goats together.

Tirzah stopped long enough to tighten her sandal strap. Before she could straighten up, she thought she saw something move on the hill to the west like a flash of metal in the red of the setting sun. Then another flash. She busied herself with her sandal, straining to see from the corner of her eye.

Shields—the metal studded shields of raiders. She could not tell how many, but with a sickening feeling in her stomach she saw that the flashes spread in a line across the brow of the hill. The raiders must surely have seen the two of them. Safety lay ahead in the camp if only they could reach it in time.

Forcing herself not to look back, she walked swiftly after Ram. She must not call out or give any sign that she had seen them.

As she caught up with him, Ram spoke sharply. "Don't point or look back," he said. "We're being watched by Bedouin."

"Then you saw them, too. What can we do, Ram?"

Ram's voice was stern. "Walk on as if you haven't seen anything. Just don't look back. Keep walking. It's our only chance to get back to the camp." With all her strength, Tirzah forced herself to look straight ahead. Her legs were wooden, but she made them move to keep pace with Ram.

As if he were out for an ordinary walk with the goats, Ram prodded them, calling to one goat, then another, to keep in line. Once he laughed a loud, long laugh, and nodded his head to her while saying between his teeth, "Keep walking, keep walking."

Tirzah wished he would be still. How else could they hear if anyone was coming behind them? If only they hadn't stayed so long at the water. They were still out of sight of the camp in this hilly, rocky place. Was Yahweh watching? She strained her eyes for the cloud.

12

War

Ram and Tirzah reached the camp safely. Runners sent to confirm the news returned quickly. They reported that a war party of Amalekites were indeed camped on the ridges near the water.

Tirzah felt a chill run down her back. She and Ram had been right under the noses of the Amalekites. They had not attacked them, probably hoping to surprise a sleeping camp later. People were hurrying in all directions, and with a start Tirzah remembered—the Amalekites were coming. Quickly she ran to help her mother and Jerioth.

For once in her life, Sorry cooperated, moving as fast as her short legs could go on the rough steep path to higher ground. Turning to look behind her, Tirzah saw old Hanna leaning heavily on Merrie's shoulder. Ahead of her, Oren swung along on his crutch as easily as the goats he drove before him. She needn't worry about him. It was Ram and her father that worried her. They had gone back to help evacuate the camp.

For some it was already too late. The Amalekites attacked the small group of stragglers, mostly elderly and sick who had stopped to camp on the other side of the water. Grief filled Tirzah's heart as word of the attack came.

At dawn the men formed their battle lines. Ram and her father, though skilled with the sling, carried the throwing spears called javelins. Their faces were grim and determined.

Man after man followed the clan leaders. Tirzah saw the men of Dan raise their prized, sickle-shaped swords as they passed where the women stood to watch them go. The sharp swords were valued because there were so few of them. If the Amalekites were well armed, how would the men of Israel stand before them? And if they lost, what then?

It would be the end of them all. She knew that the Amalekites would save alive only those who suited them as slaves. The women were already running back to the temporary camp, and Tirzah fled with them.

All day the sounds of battle shouts and clashes filled the air like a roaring wave that rose and fell to return again and again. Half a dozen times, Ram and Abishur brought wounded men back to the shelter of the tents the women had set up among the high rocks.

Tirzah shuddered at the sight of the blood-soaked men, some with pieces of javelins sticking from their bodies like giant splinters. Her mother, Jerioth, and the women without nursing children worked steadily washing and binding wounds. Old Hanna with her store of herbs was kept busy distributing and mixing her medicines.

"Tirzah, here," Jerioth called, as she covered the young man on the ground before her with a soft goatskin. The boy's face—he could not have been much older than Ram, Tirzah thought—was white, his eyes closed. Jerioth spoke softly, "Tell Hanna we have need of something for pain. We have done all we can for him."

Tirzah nodded, the great lump in her throat preventing her from speaking. She had seen the blood-reddened covering on the boy's chest. He was so young. Would he die? Quickly she hurried to the far end of the camp where Hanna knelt by a steaming pot.

On her way back with the small bowl of herbs, Tirzah saw Ram. His black hair was covered with dust, his face streaked where the sweat had run down his cheeks. This time it was an older man who slumped heavily against Ram's shoulders. Tirzah saw him hand over his burden to the strong arms of the women who came to assist him. For a minute Ram paused to wipe his forehead before he caught up with her.

"Is that water?" Ram's voice was hoarse. "I'm as parched as dry corn."

Tirzah shook her head. "Sorry, it's medicine for the wounded, but I'll get you some." Ram walked with her to where Jerioth was cleaning blood from a man's deeply gashed forehead. Putting down the bowl of herbs, Tirzah motioned Ram toward a large stone. "Sit while I fetch water."

Ram nodded. "For a moment, but hurry. I have to go back." Tirzah was quick, and Ram drank thirstily. "Ah, that helps, Tiz."

"How is the battle going?" Tirzah asked, half afraid to hear his answer.

Ram stood up. "Haven't you heard?" he asked. "Moses stands on the hill before Yahweh with his arms uplifted, and so long as he holds up his hands, our men press forward to victory. When he grows tired and lowers his arms, our men are forced to retreat before the Amalekites. Right now Aaron and Hur have put a stone beneath him to sit on, and they are holding his hands up."

Tirzah was excited. "Yahweh is helping us to fight," she said, her voice full of wonder.

"Yes, and my job is waiting. See you, Tiz." Ram hurried off, and Tirzah watched him go. Quickly she picked up the empty bowl and went back to help.

By sunset the battle was over. Joshua and the men of Israel raised a cry of victory. The Amelekites, sorely beaten, fled. Tired to the bone, every muscle aching, Ram threw himself down by the campfire. Abishur, his tunic covered with dried blood and dust, sat down beside him. "I'll sit here awhile until my legs find out that they are still attached," Abishur said, rubbing his hands with ash to clean them.

"A bowl of hot broth is what you need," Jerioth's voice soothed as she stirred the steaming contents in her cooking pot. Tirzah fetched bowls and held them for Jerioth to fill. From the first Tirzah had liked her. More and more her mother and all of them had come to depend on Jerioth's help. Dreamily, Tirzah served the boys as Jerioth hummed the song Tirzah had come to love: "I will sing to the Lord, for he has triumphed gloriously."

It had been a day to remember. Looking at Abishur's stained clothes, Tirzah thought of the wounded. Tears filled her eyes, and turning away she wiped them with the back of her hand.

Her father and Molid were coming. As they came near, Molid said, "We fought well today, Jeraheel. Sleep well tonight."

"And you," her father replied, his voice hoarse with tiredness. "Yahweh is good to his people." Both men went immediately to the tents.

One of the twins came and sat beside her. She knew it was Benj when she saw the scar on his right cheek, faded now to a small line paler than the rest of his skin.

"Here," he said, holding out his hand. On his palm was the smallest nest Tirzah had ever seen. In its center lay three tiny blue eggs. "The mother bird was killed by a stray sling shot. I found the nest under a thornbush."

Carefully, Tirzah took the little nest. "They will never hatch," she said sadly, "but how perfect the nest is." She turned it around in her hands, admiring the intricately woven twigs and thorns. "What a wonder, that a bird can make such a thing," she thought aloud.

Gently she placed the nest in Benj's hand. "Will you put it back in the thornbush? I suppose some other bird will use it before the season is past."

Benj's face was thoughtful. "I'll take it back in the morning if you like." Instantly, Tirzah saw her mistake. He had meant it as a gift to her, and she had given it back. She felt her face flush. Before she could think, Benj had risen abruptly and left, calling good-night behind him.

With a start Abishur sat up. Groggily he stared at Tirzah. "Must go home—late," he mumbled, struggling to his feet. He stumbled blindly over Ram and came dangerously close to the campfire. Tirzah sprang to her feet to pull him away to safety. He was half asleep on his feet. With her arm and shoulder supporting him, Tirzah guided Abishur on the path to his father's tent.

"Tired," Abishur muttered, leaning heavily on her arm. "Just want to lie down."

"Hang on, we're almost there," Tirzah encouraged. As they neared the tent, Abishur's mother ran toward them. "It's all right, Aunt Rebekah. He's just tired out and fell asleep by our campfire."

"Praise be to Yahweh," her aunt cried, reaching out for Abishur. Like a child he let her lead him. "I'll send someone to see you back, Tirzah, just as soon as I get Abishur to the tent."

"I'll be fine," Tirzah assured her. "I'll go now and see you tomorrow. Good-night." Before her aunt could object, she turned quickly toward her own campfire.

On the ground near it, Ram slept like a stone. A night wind blew mournfully up from the empty battle plain, making Tirzah pull her blanket close. The fire burned low, and Tirzah's eyes were heavy with sleep. Above her the Glory cloud shone softly. Yahweh had saved them.

13

Strangers

Under the blazing noon sun, small, dancing waves of heat rose from the bare ground. Sitting cross-legged in the shade of the open entry to their tent, Tirzah pulled a handful of gray wool across the carding comb. From the corner of her eye, she could see her mother resting against cushions, eyes closed, her head nodding against her chest. Nothing moved in the still air. Most of the men had gone to the far side of the camp to the tent of meeting, where Moses sat to judge disputes among the people.

Oren had stayed behind to write on the papyrus old Paser had given him. He paused in his writing. "Today Moses is going to hear Uncle Shobal's case against the men of Dan who used his ox and cart without permission. I bet I should have gone along with the others."

Tirzah hid a smile as her mother's eyes flew open to protest. "That one, may he learn before it is too late. The man has no heart, no mercy. The cart was taken to pick up the wounded. I pity those men of Dan. They should have taken anyone else's cart but Shobal's to do their good work. He was born to make trouble, that brother of mine." She sighed as she settled back against the cushions.

Tirzah added, "Uncle Shobal is determined to make them pay."

"In a war, who has time for politeness?" her mother reminded them. "Anyway, I can only hope he will be satisfied with a fair payment for his ox. Who could know an Amalekite arrow would pierce its throat?"

Tirzah stopped carding to look off toward the distant desert hills. From their tent at the north edge of camp, she could see the long horizon of empty land against the cloudless sky. Somewhere out there, small tribes of Bedouin moved about, camping where it suited them, though there was little to keep a body alive in most of that barren land.

Oren saw the small line of dark figures moving toward the camp at the same time as she did. Like tiny ants in the distance winding their way forward, a family of Bedouin was approaching.

Runners were the first to greet the strangers. But by the time the company drew near, word had spread and Moses himself came running to meet them. Tirzah stood with her mother and Oren, waiting to see who it was that had come.

As the little group passed, Moses waved and gestured toward the woman, the two young men, and the old man by his side. "My wife, my two sons, and my father-in-law have come," he shouted to all within hearing.

"Welcome, welcome indeed!" Tirzah's mother called in return. As the caravan passed, she added, "Isn't she lovely?" The woman was tall and dark-skinned. Her unveiled face revealed a straight nose, large, dark eyes, and a wide mouth whose smile showed white, even teeth. To Tirzah she was beautiful.

Moses' sons too were dark-skinned with the wiry look of those used to the hard life of the desert. From the richness of his robes, Tirzah guessed that Moses' father-in-law was a chieftain among his own people.

Jerioth had come to stand beside Tirzah, her hand resting lightly on Tirzah's shoulder. "It is good that Moses has his family with him," she said. "Even a man such as he needs the comfort of his own."

Jerioth's hand tightened gently. "Tirzah, my little dove, one day you will make a home for your own family, eh?" Tirzah felt her face grow warm. Jerioth laughed lightly. "Yes, you too will know the joy I speak of," she said.

"Shall we go and make ready for the men who will come home hungry as bears for some of our comforts?" Tirzah nodded her head and followed Jerioth.

"I'm coming too," her mother said, rising awkwardly. "Oh my, oh my, this child kicks." Tirzah ran and placed a hand on her mother's swollen stomach to feel the baby's movement, but she was too late.

Jerioth waited for them to catch up. "I think, Leah, it will be a boy from the way you carry."

"Yes, Jerioth, I think so, too. Another man-child to comfort and cook for." Her mother laughed. Tirzah bit her lip and turned her face away. She wanted a sister, not a brother this time.

At the tent of meeting a dozen or so men stood about in small groups. "Come back tomorrow," Aaron had told those who still waited for their cases to be heard. Relief eased the knot in Ram's stomach. As the three men from Dan brushed past Ram's father and his uncle Shobal, their grim faces showed no signs of softening.

Ram sighed. As family, they had all come to hear the outcome of the case. Neither his father nor any of the relatives had been able to make his uncle change his mind. He would demand full restitution and make a profit out of the business.

Shobal's face was red with anger. "An outrage, it is. All day we've waited for our turn, and just as I am called, court is dismissed." Shobal turned to Ram's father who stood nearest him. "So this is justice, impersonal, impartial justice?"

"Now, Shobal, the man's wife and children have come with his father-in-law. Surely you can't expect him not to go to them? Besides, this will give you time to think over what I've said." Ram knew that his father had tried to persuade his uncle to be satisfied with some small sum for the death of the ox.

Shobal gestured to his sons to follow and strode on ahead. It was plain that he had no intention of changing his mind. Abishur lingered just long enough to whisper to Ram: "It's no use. The ox was worth less than he wants for it, but there is nothing we can do once he makes up his mind to make a profit."

Ram gripped his friend's shoulder. "Never mind. Moses will judge wisely tomorrow, and then you can forget about the whole thing." In his heart Ram knew that peace would not come to Abishur's tent for weeks unless Shobal won his full case.

Ram watched his cousin leave, his eyes downcast, the picture of misery. I am the lucky one, he thought, turning to follow the straight back of his father. Unconsciously, Ram straightened his shoulders and matched his stride to his father's. The afternoon heat burned into his body, and he was suddenly thirsty.

It was time to fetch water, and Tirzah lifted her empty water skin, balancing it against her hip. The heat of the day was less intense now, almost pleasant, so she walked quickly. Abihail and the others would wait for her at the water. They would be full of news about the strangers since her cousins' tent was quite close to that of Moses and Miriam. When Tirzah arrived, Maacah and Abishur were among the ones who had already drawn water.

Abishur's clear, light laugh rang above Maacah's groaning complaint as the girls lifted the full waterskins. "Ooph,"

Maacah grunted. "Men should carry these things." Tirzah smiled at her. Like Ephan, Maacah was as strong as any boy her age.

"The real problem is you're bottom heavy, Maacah," Abihail teased. "As for you," she said, turning to face Tirzah, "you're becoming a turtle." Whenever Abihail teased, her eyes danced, but her tongue could bite just the same. It was the one thing about Abihail that bothered Tirzah.

She worked quickly while they talked. "Did either of you see Moses' family? I caught a glimpse of the woman as they passed."

Maacah answered at once. "Her name is Zipporah, and the boys are Gershom and Eliezer. The father-in-law is Jethro, priest of Midian." She paused for breath and was about to go on when Abihail interrupted.

"The more important thing," Abihail said in a hushed tone, "is that she's almost black. Just think of it, Moses married to a woman like that, a Midianite." Abihail stopped dramatically.

"But," Tirzah exclaimed, "she's beautiful." The woman was dark-skinned—a soft, shiny darkness, Tirzah thought, like a dark, night sky with faint stars shining in it.

"The point is, she's a Midianite," Abihail insisted. "Anyway, even if she is good-looking in a primitive way, she isn't exactly our kind of beauty."

"She's already married, so who cares about looks?" Maacah added. Tirzah grinned. Maacah's interest in beauty extended only to how much one needed to land a husband, no more, no less. In her case, she was counting on her thick, shining braid of hair to do the job.

"No, listen," Abihail protested. "I even heard some of the women saying that Miriam and Aaron are not exactly happy to see Moses' wife. They said the look on Miriam's face was downright disgust, though she hid it soon enough when the woman greeted her."

Why would Miriam and Aaron not want to see the woman, Tirzah puzzled. "What was Miriam disgusted about?"

Abihail opened her thickly lashed eyes widely. "Why, because she is a Midianite, of course. She certainly isn't one of our people. After all, Moses is our leader."

The skin was full, and Tirzah balanced it carefully as they walked back to camp. Other girls and women passed, some with empty skins, others on their way home with full ones. The chatter of voices was all around them.

Tirzah's mind drifted, and she wondered if she would see Merrie today. She had not seen the little Egyptian girl drawing water yet, but she was sure that the girl must fetch water for herself and old Hanna. A thought slipped into her head—what would Abihail think of Merrie? She brushed the question aside like a bothersome cobweb.

Abihail was bubbling over with news of the new robe her mother was making. It was a well-known fact that Abihail's mother, Ruth, was the best weaver among the women of the tribe.

Maacah sighed and smoothed the crumpled plain stuff of her robe that did nothing to hide or enhance her large figure. "Listen," she said, "tomorrow I'm making soup with meat from the conies that father found this morning. So, if you want some you had better come early or it will be gone."

Maacah was a good cook; Tirzah could vouch for that. "Maacah, old Hanna says that the way to a man's heart is through his stomach. Have you invited the twins?" she asked innocently. Maacah had already sized them up as among the possible choices for a future husband.

Maacah laughed. "Maybe I won't tell you who I am inviting." They had come to the parting of the path, and Maacah went cheerily on her way.

Abihail lingered a moment longer. "Tirzah, you know I love Abishur and no other forever. Please, please, tell me every word he says if he comes to your campfire tonight.

Mother won't hear of my leaving the tent after the evening meal. She thinks I am safe only when the sun is beating down or she is right beside me. I can hardly bear it. You are so lucky to have Abishur for a cousin."

Tirzah quickly pointed out that it was Abihail who would be lucky not to be a cousin when the time came for matchmaking.

"See you tomorrow, then," she called as Abihail left.

At the doorway of the tent, Oren still sat working on his papyrus. Tirzah put away her water jug and flung herself down beside him. As she settled herself cross-legged, Oren tossed something onto her lap. It was a small, perfectly chiseled reed pipe. She held it up to examine its leaf-pattern carving. Oren held up another identical to the one in her hands.

"Benj made them," he said. "Made one for each of us." Oren put his to his mouth and blew gently, a soft whistling note.

Tirzah's made a sound like a sick raven. Still, it was something, and maybe with practice—who knew?

"I've always wanted to play one of these," she said.

"Yes, I know," Benj's quiet voice added from behind her.

Tirzah swung round to face him. "How did you know that?"

Benj looked pleased with himself, his mouth grinning widely. "Oh, I don't know. Maybe I read your thoughts," he teased.

"Mmm. Thanks, it's great." She picked up the new pipe to try it once more. This time there was a note, and then another that she thought she recognized. While she struggled to play, Benj listened, turning his eyes up to the sky every now and then at a sour note.

When Benj left, he was grinning. She watched him moving easily down the path and wondered, How did he know I wanted a flute?

14

The Mountain of God

"So, after all these years, you, my husband, are the one chosen to be a judge over our people." Leah glowed with pride as she straightened a fold in Jeraheel's headpiece. "I always knew you were wise."

Jeraheel smiled and caught his wife about her growing waistline. "My little love, it's only as head of fifty that I am appointed. But it is a grave responsibility. I'm touched by the trust given me. On the other hand, I've had a bit of experience ruling over this household." Looking around first at Tirzah, then Ram and Oren, he drew his eyebrows into a mock frown.

"Yes, Father," Oren spoke up quickly, "and a good thing we have given you enough trouble to make you sharp." Oren ducked as his father reached a playful hand to tug at his ear.

"I must meet with the other judges this morning, good wife. Everything Moses has told us to do must be done exactly. We are to wash our clothes today and be ready for tomorrow, when Yahweh will speak from Mount Sinai. Tirzah, my dove, help your mother." He touched the tip of Tirzah's nose gently before he strode away.

"Well then, you heard your father. There is work to do," her mother said, heading for the washing sticks. Tirzah took down the basket and her spare clothes. She would wear these while the others were being washed. Ram had walked away silently, and Oren was about to follow when Tirzah grabbed the neck of his tunic.

"No, you don't," she said. "You can help with the beating, and besides, how can we wash your clothes with you still in them?"

"I wasn't going for long," Oren growled. His face flushed with anger and guilt at the half-truth. He bit his lip with frustration, trying to think of an excuse to be gone, but nothing came.

In his mind was a picture of Merrie, Paser's niece, hands protecting her face from the pebbles thrown by Chelab, the potter's son, and two other boys as she passed. Yesterday Oren had seen her drawing water at an hour when none of the other girls were near to protect her. He had no idea what he could do, but now it would have to wait.

Leah looked at her young son, frowned, and handed him a washing stick. "Change your clothes, then off with your sister, and mind you stay until all the washing is finished." Oren felt a sinking in his stomach. There would be no escape for hours yet.

• • •

In a deserted spot about a quarter mile outside the camp, Merrie sat sheltered by large overhanging rocks. She would hide until noon and then return to Hanna to fetch the washing. By that time the others, their washing done, would leave. They would be glad to go back to the cool protection of the tents from the midday heat.

She looked at her hands darkened by the sun, strong

hands. On the back of one palm was a purple bruise where one of the larger pebbles had struck her. Gently, she rubbed the spot.

The welt would heal, its color fade, but nothing would heal the fact that she was an Egyptian by birth, one of the hated people. Some of the Israelites were kind, as if they saw only the Merrie who wanted to follow Yahweh now. Others avoided her, turned their eyes away, even spoke to Hanna as if she, Merrie, were not occupying the same tent.

As for the young children like Chelab, they made their feelings well known by taunts and pebbles or anything else handy. "It isn't fair," she whispered, resting her head upon her drawn-up knees. "It isn't fair."

At the sound of a familiar greeting, Merrie raised her head. It was the Amorite who had escaped from the copper mines and joined the Hebrews as they fled Egypt. She answered gladly, the formal words of her homeland sweet to her tongue.

In a few long strides the man approached, threw his bundle of wood to the ground, and bowed his head politely. "May I join you for a rest, niece of Paser, the scribe?"

Merrie's eyes widened in surprise. "But how did you know who I was?" She had seen the man before and knew from Hanna who he was, though she had never spoken to him.

"I am Manetto, youngest son of the tomb builder Thotmos, though my mother was an Amorite. I could have stayed in Egypt and done quite well except for a quarrel that left me disowned and an exile in the Pharaoh's copper mines." His tone was bitter.

For a moment he paused, then went on speaking, his voice lighter now. "You I know from listening to the talk. You serve an old midwife and are the niece of Paser, the scribe, a former customer of Peleg, the Hebrew."

Merrie's face flushed. She should have stayed in Egypt.

Here she was a hated Egyptian, talked about so that even this stranger had heard about her. A black ant crept to the edge of her robe, and quickly she flattened it with her palm.

Manetto's large hand was even quicker. He picked up her small hand and held the bruised side to the sunlight. "So, does the old woman beat you, too?" His black eyes, deep-set between thin eyebrows, searched her face piercingly.

Merrie was uncomfortable and snatched her hand away. "No, no, Hanna does not beat me," she said. Her tongue stammered on the truth. "It is only the young boys with their pebbles. They do not just talk like their mothers and fathers." She was sorry as soon as she said it, not wanting to confide in this man. Something sinister in his eyes frightened her.

Manetto leaned closer, his voice a steely whisper. "Soon you will not have to worry about Hebrew slave children or their foolish parents."

Merrie looked at him, not understanding.

"Those of our number who left Egypt for a better life, not for some strange god, will soon leave behind this rabble of ex-slaves. Once we are safely to the north, our preparations finished, we will be on our way." Manetto placed a long finger under Merrie's chin. "You will say nothing of this to anyone, and when the time is right, you shall come with us, eh?"

Merrie's heart beat wildly. She could find no words to say. Her mind raced with conflicting thoughts—there was Hanna—that young man—and Yahweh. Would it be better to leave with her own kind, even if it meant not knowing what lay ahead?

Manetto was rising to leave. "Remember, not a word must pass those pretty lips. It would be a shame to cut out such a lovely tongue." He smiled, but the smile did nothing to soften his face. With a wave of his hand he was gone.

Merrie stood up, looking about her frantically. The sheltering rock no longer seemed safe. She was no longer safe. A tiny cry rose inside her and leapt from her lips, "Yahweh, O Yahweh, help me." Like a frightened deer, she ran back toward the camp, back to old Hanna.

In the morning Merrie took her place beside Hanna's bent form on the plain before the mountain of Yahweh, as Moses had commanded. She trembled and clung to Hanna's arm. Hanna seemed in as much fear as Merrie. Her quivering voice moaned in whispered prayer as they pressed against others also groaning in awe. It was as if they stood, all of them, like small ants terrified by the storm hovering above them.

Dense billows of smoke covered the mountaintop, yet it seemed to burn with flames beneath the cloud. Jagged streaks of lightening lit up the sky from one end to the other. Thunderclaps crashed with terrifying loudness. At the base of the mountain, a line of stones marked the boundary beyond which no man, woman, child, or beast could pass and live. Merrie shuddered. Who would dare to move one foot closer on this terrible, awful day?

Tirzah stood close to her mother and the rest of the women who clung together, their little ones clutched tightly by the hand or held in their arms. Beneath her feet, Tirzah felt the ground trembling.

Ram's mouth hung open in utter amazement as he stood with his family. His father bowed his head and pressed Oren close to his chest. As Ram stared, the tones of a trumpet coming from somewhere near the mountain grew louder and louder. Men around him were praying, some even weeping, but Ram barely heard them as he listened to a sound like nothing he had ever heard before.

All that Ram knew was that suddenly he was face down on the ground like the rest of the people around him. Only he no longer heard any other voice. He was alone in the world—Yahweh, Yahweh had come and spoken. Later, Ram could never explain how he knew, nor did he try. What happened was simply that Yahweh was there, and he knew it.

Moses alone had been called up into the mountain. When he returned, he warned the people once again not to step beyond the stones marking the edge of the mountain, but to wait for the words of God. Ram would have waited for a lifetime if need be. He knew that he would never be the same after this.

The next morning, Moses read the Book of the Covenant containing the words of the Lord to the people. "This is Yahweh's promise: You yourselves have seen what I did to Egypt, and how I carried you on eagles' wings and brought you to myself. Now if you obey me fully and keep my covenant, then out of all nations you will be my treasured possession. Although the whole earth is mine, you will be to me a kingdom of priests and a holy nation."

With one voice the people responded. "Whatever the Lord has said we shall do."

Tears rolled down Merrie's cheeks as she found herself repeating the promise to Yahweh. She would never desert him, no matter what the cost. Gently, she squeezed Hanna's old hand, and Hanna's smile lit her face with love.

Ram was among those young men chosen to bring the bulls to the altar for sacrifice. His strong arms held the halter around the bull's neck firmly, leading the animal skillfully to the priest who waited, knife in hand. The blood of the animals was caught in large bowls, their carcasses burnt. Some of the blood Moses took to pour upon the altar; the rest he sprinkled on the people as a sign of the covenant Yahweh made with them.

Overhead, the sky was clear now, the air still as if no storm had ever broken its blueness. Only the top of the mountain remained hidden in thick clouds. Tirzah sighed deeply as Aaron dismissed the crowds. Moses and his servant Joshua had gone up into the mountain once more, and the meeting was over.

What is it like to see Yahweh? she wondered. Always and always she would remember that for one moment she too had heard his voice. There were no words to describe this, but she knew.

Tirzah reached a hand to help her mother along the path. Her mother's face shone with happiness in spite of the deep dark circles beneath her eyes. It would not be long before the new baby came.

● ● ●

On the outskirts of the camp Merrie saw Manetto sitting by a campfire with a half dozen other strangers, none of them Hebrews. Had Manetto gone to the plain yesterday and today? She felt almost sure that he had not gone with the others—at least not today. How did his fire come to be so quickly ready, the pot of food already swinging above it, when others where still returning home?

She did not look long in his direction as she followed Hanna. Had he seen her? Were those piercing black eyes even now upon her? The thought worried her.

15

A Golden Idol

Oren wiped a smudge of ink from his thumb, then carefully dipped the split tip of his reed into the waterpot, touching it lightly to the dry ink. He drew another line on the papyrus stretched before him. Silently he counted. He had been right the first time. It was thirty-five days since Moses had gone up into the mountain of God. Oren rocked back on his heels to think. What should he write next?

Something was going on in the camp. He could not quite figure out what it was. His father returned from his meetings night after night with a grim look on his face. Across the room his mother sighed. Oren watched her glance at the open tent flap, frown, and return to her work. She too was worried.

Everywhere Oren went he heard stories about the fate of Moses, who seemed to have disappeared. Some of them were as eerie as any of old Paser's tales had been. There was talk of choosing new leaders. Where was Moses? Oren wondered.

This morning he had walked out to look at the mountain. Anyone could see that the cloud still sat covering its top.

Maybe tomorrow Moses would return. He would be glad to add that to his book of their travels.

His gift of ink from Paser was almost gone. Gently, he stirred the small bit of thick sediment that was left. If only he knew what to add that would keep the supply going. Paser had known. A picture of Paser sitting in his garden, papyrus in hand, passed through his mind. Merrie? Would Merrie know how to replenish the ink? Carefully, he packed his tools away and picked up his crutch. He would find Merrie and ask her.

Sadly, Merrie rubbed a bit of the ink between her thumb and forefinger. "I know only that it was a metallic substance my uncle used to mix with the charcoal. How or where he got it, I do not know."

With the look of someone who just had an idea, Merrie wiped her fingers and reached for a piece of goatskin. "You could use this for parchment. I can scrape the hair from the skin for you, and the ink for it is easy to make."

Oren fingered the goatskin. It would do. "If the ink works, it will be fine," he said.

Merrie was already scraping away at the skin on her lap. "All we need for the ink is right here," she said. "One mixes charcoal and oil, though the exact amount is important." It took a bit of doing, but by the time Oren left, he was satisfied that the new ink would work.

Merrie watched him go, then hurried to pick up her waterskin. Already the sun was beginning to weaken. No one would be at the water now. The shadows were lengthening as she finished filling the bag.

She walked quickly, anxious not to be caught on the path in the dark. By now Hanna would be home and wondering about her. She had spent too long with the boy. The sight of him had brought back bittersweet memories from the past. Her uncle had really loved the child.

Without warning, Manetto interrupted her thoughts.

Merrie gasped as he stepped into the path no more than three feet ahead of her.

"Sorry, little one, sorry. I did not mean to startle you." Manetto held his hands palm up in a gesture of apology. "You were deep in thought and perhaps did not hear me coming?"

"No, I didn't hear you," Merrie answered, forcing a calmness that she did not feel into her voice. "Please, let me pass. I am already late and will be missed."

Manetto stepped aside quickly so that she could go ahead. "Go and fulfill your duties tonight as usual. But soon you will see who are the true masters."

Merrie's instinct was to hurry past him. Instead, she looked searchingly at him. "I do not know what you mean," she said.

Manetto smiled that peculiar cold smile Merrie hated. "The god of the Hebrews no longer sends his priest. He has tired of this rabble of slaves. It is time for the power of the old gods once more. Those of us who knew them best shall be their trusted servants."

Merrie shrank back from the man. Yahweh would never allow such a thing.

Manetto grinned. "What do you fear, daughter of Nut?"

Merrie turned her eyes from his face. Nut was Egypt's goddess of the sky.

"Never fear, little one. Manetto will see that you are well treated. Now go before Khonsu rises and spots you."

Merrie hurried past him, not slowing her pace nor stopping to look back. Khonsu was the moon god. She had heard stories of his affairs, none of them pleasing to her. This talk of the old gods in the camp of Yahweh frightened her. Above her the moon was indeed rising, and Merrie stumbled in her haste, splashing a bit of the water over her sandals.

As she straightened and steadied the water skin, she saw

the shining cloud of Yahweh still above the mountain beyond the camp. "Yahweh watches over his people," she thought and sighed. Whether for relief or wonder at the great mystery of Yahweh, she didn't know. Ahead, the light of Hanna's campfire welcomed her with dancing, yellow brightness.

• • •

Two days later, Merrie, her hands bound tightly behind her back, wept bitterly with longing for old Hanna and her welcoming campfire. Everywhere fires of rebellion burned in the camp. People seemed to have gone mad.

Huge bonfires flamed far into the night while men and women danced about them wildly, some of them drunkenly. Women prepared food as for a great feast, and people donned their finest clothing. At the remote eastern edge of the camp, the strangers among the Hebrews had their tents. There Merrie sat on the ground before Manetto's tent watching the madness.

Is this happening in all of the camp? she wondered. It was no use to struggle. Her wrists burned where the twisted vines binding them rubbed into her skin. If only she could free her hands, she could untie her feet from the stake Manetto had driven into the ground.

The thought of his cruel smile made her squirm with anger. She had fought against his powerful grip, tooth and nail. Why, why had she gone again for water late in the evening when there was no one to help her? She should have known after Manetto's first visit that something like this could happen. She had seen the look of surprise, then anger on Manetto's face when she refused to go with him.

"I follow Yahweh now. Can't you see? There is his cloud still on the mountain," she had said, pointing.

For a minute, Manetto had hesitated. "So, you still think

safety lies with these slaves. I will soon convince you how wrong you are, and then you will serve me, little sister." He had carried her off like a sack of grain, ignoring her struggles, one large hand covering her mouth.

Merrie licked her dry lips. All that was changed now. Manetto no longer tried to reason with her. There was no need now that the whole camp was bent on finding a new god to lead them. Manetto could choose a wife from those women who seemed to hang on his every word. They followed him about as if he were a god.

This afternoon two of them had painted her face and dressed her in garlands of flowers. "You must be beautiful for the new god," one of them said.

"What new god? I belong to Yahweh," Merrie cried out.

The women had laughed. "Just be patient," the other said. "Soon you will see our new god. He is all golden. You'll love him, you'll see." The woman's voice was wobbly, her breath sour with the smell of wine. When they left Merrie wished she had begged them for a drink of water. Her face felt dry and heavy with paint, and her throat ached from the sobs that wrenched her.

They would come for her when the sun set, to take her to the new god. Horror filled her mind. If only Manetto would return before then; she would promise him anything to escape. The light was beginning to change, and still he had not come.

"O help me, Yahweh. Please help me," she prayed. Nothing moved among the deserted tents. From somewhere on the north side of the camp, sounds of revelry carried on the air. Merrie closed her burning eyes.

Had she fallen asleep? Was that Ram coming towards her? It was Ram.

"Oh, help me, Ram, help me," she cried.

"Is it really you?" Ram asked. "What have they done to you?" Without waiting for an answer, he went to work on the vines that bound Merrie's feet. "We've been looking everywhere for you, for two days, ever since Hanna couldn't find you. This was the last place I thought of to look. It was just a chance idea that made me come here."

Merrie held Ram's arm for a moment as she stood on her cramped legs. "I would not leave Yahweh, but Manetto brought me here thinking to persuade me. They want to sacrifice me to their new god." She tore the garlands from her neck. "Oh Ram, what will we do?"

The peculiarly marked and painted face of Merrie was eerie, but Ram could see fear in her eyes. "We run," he said. Taking her hand he headed west. Merrie ran for her life, the blood coming back into her feet and legs like sharp knives.

"My father and some of the others have gone into the hills west of camp," Ram said, his breath coming hard. "He and Molid went down to the camp to reason, but they were outnumbered by the mobs. When the violence began, those who feared Yahweh fled to the hills. We'll be safe there."

Ram glanced behind him as they ran. Any moment they could be pursued. They had to reach cover.

In a thick shelter of rocks, they stopped to rest. "It's not far now," Ram assured Merrie as he leaned his back against a rock. They had reached the first hill, and Ram could see no sign of anyone following them. Merrie sat on the ground and let her head droop against her drawn-up knees. Suddenly she began to rub her face with both hands. Jumping up, she looked about frantically. Ram sat up in alarm.

"I can't let anyone see me like this," Merrie said half to herself. The small, white flowers of a nearby broom bush caught her eye. In a moment she was tearing off handfuls of the sweet fragrant blooms to wipe the thick paint from her skin. When she finished, she was once more the plain-faced Merrie that Ram knew, her face red from the rubbing, but clean.

As they approached the small plateau, well hidden from

the valley below, Tirzah ran from one of the tents to meet them. Impulsively, she threw her arms around Merrie.

"You've found her," she cried out. Standing back from Merrie, Tirzah searched the girl's face. "You are all right, aren't you, Merrie?" she asked.

Merrie could not control the tears that ran down her cheeks. "I am safe. I could not go with Manetto and the others because I promised to follow Yahweh. They were going to give me to their new god."

She covered her eyes for a moment, then went on. "Oh Tirzah, I prayed to Yahweh for help, and then Ram came." Some of the women gathered around, and now kind hands gently led Merrie toward the tents.

Tirzah stayed behind with Ram. "Where did you find her, Ram?"

Ram sat down on the ground, suddenly tired. "She was in the entryway to Manetto's tent, tied to a stake in the ground and dressed for sacrifice to the new god." He remembered Merrie's strangely painted face, the garlands of flowers, the clothing, and shuddered to think of what might have been.

Tirzah put a hand on Ram's shoulder. "Whatever comes, Ram, I'm glad you are my brother." Ram looked at his sister, her slim frame, the bright intelligence of her eyes so like their father's.

"It's going to be all right, Tiz. We'll stick together," he said.

"Look, Ram, up there." Tirzah pointed to the top of the great mountain rising above all the other hills. "See, Yahweh's cloud is still there."

Ram stared at the cloud glowing with fiery light as the night came on. "We must just wait and see, Tiz, wait and see."

During the second watch of the night, Ram took his turn along with Abishur and his uncle Caleb, watching the narrow pass to the plateau. From the valley they could hear the shouts and music of celebration. "It's a terrible thing they do," his uncle said quietly. "The people laid their earrings and necklaces at Aaron's feet and got him to melt them down."

His uncle's voice trembled, "What came from the fire was a thing of evil in the shape of a bull-calf. Now they are calling it the god who brought them out of Egypt."

Ram shivered in the cold night air. In the far distance Yahweh's cloud still glowed about the mountain top. "Yahweh brought us out of Egypt," he said, "and I will stand against any man who says otherwise."

His uncle patted his arm, and Abishur's too. "Good lads, both of you. We will watch sharp this night. Yahweh is not done with his people, though I fear his anger will fall on many."

The night passed slowly till it was the third watch, and Ram gladly gave his place to his father and Molid. Wearily, he stumbled back to the tent, flung himself down, and was asleep instantly.

In a nearby tent Merrie snuggled close to old Hanna, who slept peacefully, a smile on her face. She was so glad that I am back, thought Merrie. Tenderly she pulled the robe up about Hanna's shoulders. Hanna would never let Manetto take her. A nagging fear rose to taunt her, but she shut her eyes tightly and let herself drift into sleep.

16

One Small Miracle

Tirzah woke from sleep to the sound of birds singing in the acacia trees close to the tent. Lazily, she kept her eyes shut, only to open them instantly as a cry burst onto the morning stillness. "Moses is coming down from the mountain. Joshua is with him. Hurry, come." Tirzah was up instantly.

Leaving everything behind them, the entire camp ran to meet their leader. Tirzah and her mother were hurrying too when her mother gasped and stood still. Her hand tightened on Tirzah's shoulder.

"It's no use," her mother said. "I can't make it." She had already turned pale as she stood bent over with pain.

Tirzah felt her own stomach knot and a chill run down her spine.

"Jeraheel, you must go down with Ram and Oren along with the others. Tirzah and I will stay here," her mother said, gasping for breath. "Tirzah, run and catch Jerioth quickly.

"I will not leave you here alone, my love," Jeraheel said firmly, as he placed a strong arm about his wife to support her. "Bring Jerioth, and Ram, see that you stay with your uncle Caleb. Oren, stick with your brother. I will come when I can."

When Tirzah came running with Jerioth, her mother was already inside the tent. Gently, Jerioth touched Tirzah's arm. "Tirzah, you must keep the fire going, and wait for me outside the tent." She patted Tirzah and quickly went inside, closing the tent flap behind her.

Tirzah stirred the fire and tended it till it glowed brightly once again. She sat back on her heels and listened for any sound within the tent. Would the baby be all right? Would her mother suffer much? Her eyes filled with tears. She felt suddenly alone in the big world.

When her father returned with an armful of wood for the fire, she looked up at him. "Father, will she die?"

In one great stride her father scooped her up in his arms like a little child, letting her burrow her head into his strong shoulders. "Yahweh is good. Whatever he wills is right. Now, little bird, you must wait patiently as I did when you were born, and before that with Ram, and again with Oren. You and I can do nothing to hurry the coming of a little one. They make their entrance in their own time."

He set her down and dried her eyes with the edge of his robe. "There is something I want you to do," he said. "A little while ago I fed the goats and Sorry. I have not seen such a sight as that donkey's hide in a long while. How about grooming her?" He smiled down at Tirzah. "You are the only one she will allow near long enough to do a good job."

Tirzah hesitated, looking toward the tent and then to the far side of the hill where the animals were. Her father shook his head. "Come now, you must not worry. I will be here with your mother. These things take a long time. I promise to call you; now go."

Impulsively she kissed her father's large sun-browned hand. "You are a good father," she whispered and, without looking up, ran gratefully to tend Sorry.

All morning she commanded and cajoled, trying to get Sorry to cooperate. "You'd better not try that again," she said, rubbing her shoulder where Sorry had nipped it. Sorry turned her head away as if she had no idea what Tirzah meant. Twice the donkey had sent Tirzah backward, combs and all, while she deliberately rolled herself in dust.

At noon her father brought her food. There was no news yet, but now Tirzah had something to give Sorry for a bribe. Within the hour she finished the job, leaving Sorry clean and contentedly munching the last of Tirzah's bread.

By the time her father came again, Tirzah had braided the silky hair of two goats, decorated the baby goats with broom bush flowers which they ate, and was thinking of what to do with the ram. One glance at her father's face told her that something was wrong.

He looked strained and weary, as if the strength had drained from him. His eyes were far away for a moment before he spoke. "The child is a girl, a small one. Jerioth thinks it will yet be well with her, but it is too soon to tell."

"And Mother—how is she?" Tirzah asked.

"Perhaps the trouble of these last few days, the hardness of the journey. . . . I don't know. She is very tired. It has been a long day. I will call you as soon as Jerioth says you may see her." Tirzah had taken his hand in hers and held it tightly.

He looked at her gently. "We must both pray. Yahweh's will is best." Tirzah watched him go, her heart too heavy to pray.

At sunset the others returned for one more night in the little camp. Tirzah sat outside the tent, still waiting for her father and Jerioth to call her inside where her mother lay so ill.

Ram and Oren sat huddled close to the fire, their faces full of grief. Benj and Reuben had come to hear the news and gone quietly away with their father to their own tent. Old Hanna was with her mother, too, and Merrie sat like a small shadow at the edge of the firelight, waiting for her.

Slowly, stopping to choose his words carefully, Ram told them what had taken place in the camp below. "Moses was so angry that he broke the tablets of stone from Yahweh, crying out that the people were not worthy of them. Then he had Joshua grind up the golden calf and sprinkle the powder on the water. He made the people drink the bitter water to remind them of Yahweh's wrath."

Ram paused to brush a fly from his face. "I can barely tell you what happened next. Moses called for those who were for the Lord to stand by him. There were many besides us, mostly Levites." Ram cleared his throat. "But it was the Levites with their swords that Moses commanded to go back and forth through the camp, slaying brother, friend, and neighbor who had not come to the Lord's side." Ram stopped.

Tirzah lifted her head to look at him with amazement. "Then that was the terrible noise we heard today. Father said that it must have something to do with Yahweh's punishment when Moses saw what the people were doing." Scenes of the wounded from the Amalekite raid flashed before her. But this, this killing in the camp, she could not picture.

Ram shook his head as if to clear it. "Never, never have I heard or seen anything like it. Tonight there is mourning all over the camp. I can hardly believe what has happened and that we are spared." He looked at Merrie. "Manetto also is dead."

From the shadows where she sat, Merrie spoke quietly. "Yahweh is very great. He could have punished us all. In Egypt the priests do not teach about the mercy of the gods, only their terrible anger."

Oren nodded in agreement. "Right. Anyone could see that Yahweh's cloud still covered the mountain. They should have waited for Moses." He was interrupted by his father's appearance in the doorway of the tent. Every face turned expectantly.

"Your mother is sleeping peacefully, thanks be to Yahweh."

A sigh of relief escaped from Tirzah's lips, only to leave her heart beating wildly at the unasked question: What of the baby?

As if he had heard, her father nodded his head. "The child too sleeps, and if Yahweh wills, she shall live. Tomorrow you will see them."

Tirzah felt as if a fresh breeze swept over her. Tomorrow she would see her new sister. Her mother was all right. Moses had returned, and life would go on. All would be well.

"Tirzah," Ram said, breaking into her thoughts, "there is something else I must tell you. Our uncle Shobal is dead. He died at the hand of a Levite neighbor."

Tirzah's heart jumped. "Abishur, what about Abishur?"

"Abishur is well. Jonathan too, only their father is dead," Ram answered. "But they grieve for their father."

"Yes," Tirzah whispered, "they must be grieving for their father." She too would mourn for him, for the uncle she had known as a child. He had been good to her in spite of his shortcomings.

The night air felt chill, and Tirzah pulled her mantle closer. "Oh, Uncle Shobal, why did you go against Yahweh?" she mourned. The sound of a tiny cry like a kitten's came from inside the tent, reminding Tirzah of the new life, the little sister she had always wanted. In spite of her sadness for Abishur's family, a warm, soft feeling flowed over her as she listened to the baby's crying.

17

Hanna

No one left the small camp in the hills. On the following day Joshua had come with news of plague in the camp. The sickness was everywhere, fever and boils. For some death came quickly. Until it was over, Joshua advised them to stay where they were. Only Hanna offered to go down to the camp and nurse the sick. Reluctantly, Joshua gave in to the old woman and waited for her to gather her medicines.

Inside the tent, Merrie fell to her knees before Hanna. "Please, my mother, do not go down, I beg you," she pleaded. "Surely Yahweh has sent this plague as a punishment. Do not go, I beg you."

Gently, Hanna pried the girl's hands from her robe. "Now child, Yahweh may punish those who do wrongly, but when a man or woman is down sick we must not add to their suffering by refusing help. Yahweh has given us herbs and plants to use for the good of all. I must use my skill wherever it is needed." Hanna turned and reached for her potions, placing each packet carefully into her bag.

Merrie rose to her feet. "I want to go with you and help you," she insisted.

"No, child. I cannot expose you to the sickness." Hanna spun around to face Merrie, her eyes softening as they sought the girl's. "You are young, with all life before you. I have lived a long life. I am ready to go. Now let me get on with my packing or young Joshua will grow weary of waiting for me."

"Please, let me go with you," Merrie begged. "I'm strong. I know how to mix the medicines for you. You will need me." Once more she grasped Hanna's arm tightly. "Don't you see, Mother, I cannot let you go alone? Take me with you, and I will serve those Yahweh has stricken too."

Hanna's eyes filled with tears as she patted Merrie's hand. "You are a precious daughter to me. Come then, if you will. Get your things quickly." Relieved, Merrie threw her arms about Hanna's neck and hugged her.

Merrie was not prepared for the stench of sickness that fouled the air as soon as they entered the first tent. Hanna bent over a woman and child, both burning with fever. The woman's body was covered with boil-like sores that oozed. The child had a few angry red sores that had not yet broken. Hanna showed Merrie how to make compresses and apply them.

Softly, Merrie laid a wet cloth on the child's chest. She touched the little one's forehead, smoothing the dark hair from her face. As she did, the child opened her eyes wearily, then closed them again. Merrie went on cooling the fevered body with water mixed with fever herbs. When Hanna came to dose the child, Merrie lifted the hot head and held it while Hanna administered the medicine.

Hanna wiped the last sore clean and laid a compress on the mother's chest. She had done all she could, at most making the woman more comfortable. With a sigh, she motioned for Merrie to come and lifted the tent flap. All Hanna's skill would not save the mother, but perhaps the child would yet live.

Outside the tent a neighbor woman waited for them, a look of woe on her face. "Both her sons and her husband are gone. What will the poor things do?" she wailed.

Hanna handed her a small jar of medicine. "Mix one part of the medicine with two of water, and give them each a dose at sunset. If the woman lives, do it again in the morning," Hanna said.

"Mercy on us all. Then the poor woman will not live?" the woman cried.

"It is not likely," Hanna replied. "I don't even know if the child will survive. I'm sorry, but there's nothing more I can do here, and others are waiting."

Abruptly Hanna followed a young girl who stood ready to guide her to her family's tent, where the rest of the family lay stricken. As Merrie walked behind them, she wondered if the child would live, and if it did, who would care for the tiny thing?

They had taken no time to rest or eat, and already the sun was going down. Wearily, Merrie stumbled from the last tent into the dimming light. Behind her, Hanna lingered to watch an old man cough and wipe the blood from his chin.

It seemed endless to Merrie, tent after tent filled with people who lay too ill to help themselves or even move. When Hanna finally came, Merrie silently took her bag. Together they went to the tent Joshua had set aside for them.

Long before the light of dawn, Hanna was up heating water and mixing fresh potions of herb medicines. Merrie bit her lip as she struggled up from a deep sleep. She wanted to scold Hanna and tell her that she must get her rest. Instead, she crawled slowly from her blanket into the cold predawn air.

When they were out of medicine, Hanna sent Joshua for more. In other parts of the camp, other women like Hanna worked as she did to save those they could. There were just too many sick, too few to help, and little that could be done for the desperately ill. Each day the death toll mounted. Merrie wanted to shut her ears to the sounds of wailing mourners and close her eyes to the sight of oozing sores and dying flesh.

On the fifth day, there were no new cases for Hanna to treat. On the seventh day there were no more deaths. As people grew better, they helped one another. It was over, and Hanna was no longer needed. At last they could return to their own tent.

Merrie watched while Hanna rested. They had only gone a little way up the hill when Hanna stopped the first time. Her breath came in little gasps. "I'll be all right in a minute, child, just a minute of rest," Hanna had said. And she had been better, or so it seemed. Now Merrie was frightened.

Hanna's pale face was shiny with cold sweat. Her body sagged heavily like a partly filled sack of grain. She sat on the ground, leaning her head against her drawn-up knees. When Merrie sat at her feet, Hanna looked up with eyes encircled by dark shadows.

"You are worn out," Merrie said. "I should not have let you climb the hill until you rested another day." Her hands chafed Hanna's cold ones. "Rest now, and I will watch till you wake," she said.

Hanna smiled weakly and let Merrie ease her gently back down on the ground, her head against Merrie's bundle. "You are a good child. Yahweh is good. I am an old woman who should know better than I do what things an old body can do." She closed her eyes and murmured, "Yes, rest. I will rest while you watch."

Merrie did not know when Hanna had slipped quietly away. It must have been after she had made a little shelter over Hanna's head to shield her from the sun. Time passed, but Merrie could not tell how much or when. She sat holding the old hand in hers, feeling the stiffness that was already setting in. She was still sitting, holding Hanna's lifeless hand, when the twins found her.

She saw them and she heard them, but it was as if they were outside her world. She was a shadow, they were real. When Benj tried to loosen her hold on Hanna's hand, she pushed him away with her other hand. They were pleading with her, but if she had a voice, she did not know where it had gone. There was nothing to say.

They must have gone away, because for a long while she sat in the stillness. The sun beat down on her, making the shadow that she was feel its scorching fury. She could not feel anything else, only the heat.

Egyptians feel heat, she thought. If Yahweh sent the sun, then it must be good. If Yahweh sends his sun to me, why do Yahweh's children throw stones? They had hurt her, those little boys with their stones.

Now there was no place to go. Her head felt as if a hot knife were cutting into it. She was puzzled. Were there two of her? One an Egyptian? Who was the other one? She tried to see past the dizzying heat that blinded her.

Someone was holding her head to keep her from drowning. She could feel the cold waters closing over her body, and a voice crying out with pain. Jerioth placed a cooling cloth on Merrie's forehead. Tirzah, wincing as Merrie cried out, continued to wipe the girl's arms and chest with a mixture of water and fever herb.

"Her forehead feels a bit cooler to me," Jerioth said softly. "I think the fever is coming down."

Sitting back on her heels, she watched Tirzah. "My little bird, I do believe that you have the heart of a healer. You have been bathing her for hours now. Shall I let you rest a while?"

Tirzah paused for a moment to reply. "No thanks. I really love helping. Besides, I let her rest often. The water feels so cold to her skin that she cries out when it first touches her."

Tirzah smoothed the light cover across Merrie's chest.

"At least there is no sign of plague, just fever," she said.

Jerioth took the cloth that was beginning to warm and replaced it with a cool one. "No, I do not think there is any danger of plague. The child was in the sun too long, probably worn out with grief and hard work in the camp."

Tirzah nodded her head in agreement. "Poor old Hanna. Joshua said she saved the lives of many." A tear rolled down Tirzah's cheek, and she brushed it away quickly. "I'll miss her, dear old thing. I wish she could have gone all the way to the Promised Land, don't you?"

Jerioth's eyes were full, a look of tender love on her face. "Yes, little bird. I will miss her too. But I think she has already gone to the Promised Land."

Tirzah thought of Moses' words at the funeral. High above the mourners a lone bird had caught her attention. Watching it circle, then hang floating in the air before it flew off toward the west, she heard only snatches of Moses' prayer, but those lines had settled in her memory. She could hear them now.

"Yahweh, you have been our dwelling place throughout all generations. Before the mountains were born or you brought forth the earth and the world, from everlasting . . . you are God." Tirzah held the damp cloth lightly as her lips formed the words. "Satisfy us in the morning with your unfailing love, that we may sing for joy and be glad all our days." Maybe for Hanna it was like morning. The thought was too big to hold for long.

Merrie stirred and Tirzah placed the cloth against Merrie's forehead. Though it seemed somehow right for Hanna to die at an old age, Tirzah did not want Merrie to follow her.

18

Benj's Stone

How could sheep be so dumb? Ram pulled the thick black thorn from the side of his hand and put the stinging hand to his mouth. At his feet on the floor of the dry wadi, a fat sheep stood nosing about for food. It was covered with dust and bits of thorn bush tangled in the curly wool, but none the worse for its wandering off from the others. For an hour Ram had searched for it, at last hearing its silly bleating.

With a swish of his rod, he drove it along the gully bottom, back toward the flock he had left behind with Reuben. It was hot, and Ram could feel the sweat running down his back. The sheep must have slid its way into the wadi and then continued walking in it to have come so far.

He brushed a brown lizard from his path and watched it slip quickly into a crevice. The sheep took no notice, stopping when he stopped, moving on when he moved. At a bend in the wadi, the sheep bounded out of sight, and Ram hurried after it, only to stop short at the sight in front of him.

It was Abishur. He was sitting on a flat stone under the overhanging bank of the stream. For a minute they both stared at each other. It had been a week since the funeral, but Abishur still had not spoken a word about his father's death.

Now Abishur gestured to another stone. "Be my guest," he said.

Ram sat down. "How long have you been out here?" he asked.

Abishur picked up his flute, but put it down again. "Oh, no more than an hour or two. I left the flock with Jonathan. He is the practical one, anyway." Abishur's voice was bitter. "Practical, wasn't that what they called my father?" Ram was silent.

Abishur put his flute to his mouth and this time played a mournful tune, one Ram had heard before. "I wasn't there when he died, you know. Jonathan was with him, but not me. I was up in the hills, safe and secure."

"You couldn't have helped him, anyhow," Ram said. "Your father was a leader. The Levites knew that. I'm sorry. He believed he was right. You couldn't have changed that."

Abishur picked up a small stone and sent it dashing along the wadi bottom. "I didn't try. Maybe if I had tried to help him, something would have changed." Abishur turned his head away from Ram.

Ram reached out a hand to his cousin, "Look, if it's any help, I know something about guilt. I once followed your father and Jonathan without question. If Yahweh hadn't done a miracle at the sea that day, we might have died together fighting the Egyptians."

Abishur made no sign that he had heard, and Ram withdrew his hand.

"Listen, I know you feel that you failed him somehow. I felt that way, too, like I'd failed my own father, and Moses and Yahweh too." The sheep nuzzled between Ram's feet, and he pushed it away. "Do you know what I mean, Abishur?"

Abishur answered quietly. "I know what you are getting

at, but there is a difference. My father is dead. Yours is still alive."

Ram bowed his head in his hands because it was true. At least he had been given a second chance. How could he help his friend, his cousin?

"Only Yahweh knows what might have been," he said. "You did what was right before Yahweh. Can a man do more?"

A deep groan wrenched Abishur as if it had come from the soles of his feet. "When we were little, he loved us. He was good to us." His voice broke as he whispered, "I loved him. I would have died for him."

Like a brother, Ram held Abishur's shaking frame close. When his sobs quieted, Ram sat quietly by. Their words were few, but after a while Ram knew that Abishur was ready to return. Together they rose and headed toward the camp.

Halfway there, Benj met them, the hides of three coneys strung on a stick across his shoulder. The coneys were full grown, with long, black whiskers and broad nails on each toe for digging. They were not much larger than rabbits and hard to catch. How had Benj managed three at once?

Proudly, Benj pointed to the coneys. "Good eating," he said.

Ram admired the black-and-brown skins, highly valued for their durability.

Benj looked questioningly at Ram. "Want to trade? Three skins for a goatskin?"

Ram laughed. "Thanks, I wish I could, but all our spare skins have gone to be used on the new tabernacle."

Moses had received instructions for making each part of the tabernacle walls, roof, and furnishings. Every day the people brought gifts to be used for the building. Ram had given his arm bands to be melted down for their copper. He had been amazed at the heaps of gold, silver, copper, colored yarns, goatskins, and sea-cow skins piling up for the work ahead.

Benj turned to Abishur. Before he could ask, Abishur answered. "Ours too. Sorry. Come back in about a month, and we'll see."

"Mm," Benj grunted, hoisting his catch higher on his shoulder.

"You are quite the hunter," Abishur said, fingering one of the pelts. It was true. Coneys lived in groups of fifty or more, with a system of guard coneys who whistled a warning at the approach of danger. A hunter would have to be quick to catch even one before they scurried into the rocks.

Benj fell into step with the others. He was proud of his catch. It had been a good day. Coneys weren't all that he'd found. He said nothing of the bag tied to his belt. Time enough for that later, after he had shown it to Tirzah.

As they entered the camp, Abihail joined them. Ever since the funeral, she kept turning up with little offerings of sympathy. She was still bringing honeycakes, though they seemed to be meant more for Abishur than the rest of the family.

This time she held out a small bowl. "A bit of stew," she said lightly. "I made it myself. I hope you like it." Her long lashes fluttered shyly.

Abishur smiled, taking the bowl from her hands. It was small, just enough for one person. "I'm sure my mother will love it," he teased. Instantly her eyes grew wide with shock.

"But," he continued, "if you don't mind, I'm starving and shall eat it myself." Blushing, Abihail laughed her silvery laugh.

Ram grinned and thumped his cousin's shoulder heartily. "Some people have all the breaks," he said. Turning to Abihail, he made a small mock bow. "Fair One, should you desire to have another test your cooking skill, I am at your service."

Before he could duck, Abihail gave a strong pull to his headpiece. "I do not cook for bears," she said, turning to run lightly away. She did not stop to chat with Tirzah, who was just coming to where the little group stood.

Tirzah put down her empty basket and ran her fingers lightly over the coney skins. Abishur and Ram were already on their way to the tents. Tirzah looked up to see Benj staring at her, his dark eyes dancing with flecks of light.

"Nice, eh?" he said. Tirzah only nodded and picked up a long set of whiskers hanging from one of the hides. Benj fished in the pouch at his belt with his free hand. "I have something else to show you, Tiz. Look here." In his hand was a large flat stone.

Tirzah took the stone, curious to inspect the grooves she saw imprinted on its side. "Why, it's a fish, the whole body of a fish."

"Right, bones and all," Benj said. "And see there on the side, a sea shell embedded in the rock."

"Where in the world did you find it?" Tirzah asked.

Benj scratched his head as he answered. "That's the funny part. You can tell that the shell got caught in the rock somehow, and I think the fish did too, it's so perfect. What I'd like to know is, how did that rock get attached to the top of a hill in the middle of the desert?"

Tirzah held the whitish rock carefully, turning it first one way, then another. "What will you do with it?" she asked.

Benj looked surprised. "Didn't you know? It's yours, of course."

Now it was Tirzah's turn to be surprised. "I shouldn't keep it, Benj. It's too wonderful." She held the rock in both hands, wanting it, yet unsure what to do.

Benj settled the matter. "Take it. I meant you to have it. Besides, there are probably others. Next time I go hunting up there, I'll look around for more."

They had begun walking slowly toward camp, Tirzah

with the rock in her basket. Benj kept the coney skins on the shoulder farthest from Tirzah. Already they were beginning to smell badly and would get worse before they were cured.

All evening Tirzah kept the rock a secret. When everyone was seated around the fire, she brought it out and passed it around. When it came to Molid, he looked at it a long while.

"This is a sign," he said finally, glancing at Benj. "A sign of the great flood that once covered the hill and left this behind until you found it today, son."

Her father spoke up from the shadows of the fire. "I have heard Moses tell the story of our ancestor Noah and the great flood, but it would please me to hear it again, Molid, if you would tell it."

When Molid finished, a feeling like awe and peace mixed together filled Tirzah's mind. How great Yahweh was.

19

A New Way

From where she sat in the small circle of students, Tirzah could see the mottled skin on the teacher's hand as it held his teaching stick. She tried to listen to the words so that she could repeat them with the others. It was all so new, so wonderful, learning the words from Yahweh. She could not imagine what life was like before. Now everyone must learn the commandments, even the children.

The teacher's stick rapped for attention. "Repeat after me," he said, "everyone together.

You shall not misuse
   the name of the Lord your God,
For the Lord will not hold anyone guiltless
   who misuses his name.

Tirzah said the words haltingly at first, then louder along with the other voices raised in unison with the teacher's.

"Good, good," the teacher commended them. "Now go along home, and remember your lesson."

Tirzah walked slowly. It was already hot, the sky above

her a brilliant blue except for the cloud of Yahweh hanging low in the distance, right above the new tabernacle. It was always there.

When the cloud moved, Moses said, they would follow it as before. Tirzah tried to picture how it would be. First, the newly built ark of Yahweh, beautiful and so holy that only the priests could bear it on special carrying poles. Then, the tabernacle with all its parts carried by the Levites. And last, the people would come marching by tribes behind the leaders.

It was such a glorious picture in Tirzah's mind that she imagined she could hear the new silver trumpets sounding the call. But it was only Abishur striding along the path playing a lively song on his flute. She waited for him to catch up.

Taking the flute from his lips, he smiled his old smile. With his sun-browned skin, he was handsomer than ever. Tirzah fell into step beside him. "That's a new song," she said. "I like it."

"A new song for a new day, Tiz."

"A hot one," Tirzah commented. The sun was almost directly above them.

"That's not exactly what I meant," Abishur said. "Everything's changed, Tiz. We're a nation now, the People of the Covenant. We have the laws of Yahweh for living rightly. It's a whole new way of life, a good one."

A stone wedged itself in Tirzah's sandal, and she stopped to pick it out. She hadn't thought of all those things, and she liked the sound of People of the Covenant.

"I know," she said. "Today we learned the commandment to honor our father and our mother, so that we may enjoy long life in the Promised Land."

Immediately she was sorry she'd mentioned it to Abishur. "I didn't mean to make you think about your father," she said weakly.

"It's okay, Tiz. I'm over all that now." His tone was calm

and quiet. "Besides, we learn the same commandments of Yahweh in our group." Abishur and the older boys met separately with one of the elders.

They had come to the dividing of the path, and Abishur stood for a minute, looking at Tirzah. "Don't ever grow up, Tiz," he said. With a light tap of his flute on the tip of her nose, he left her.

His remark stung her. She was not a child, and just because he was a cousin was no reason for him to treat her like one. Under her breath Tirzah muttered, "And I suppose you're grown up?" It made no sense even as she said it.

Striding down the path and playing his flute, Abishur couldn't hear her anyway. She wished he had. Abihail was hardly older than she was. Let him try telling her she's a child.

She stormed into the tent just as little Deborah woke from her nap. Her blue eyes were open wide, and she smiled and cooed as she recognized Tirzah. Her tiny arms reached out to be picked up. Tirzah felt all her hostility melt away before this perfect little sister. "You dear, you precious love," she crooned softly.

When Leah entered the tent and saw her two girls together, pride and love swelled within her. Yahweh is good, she thought, putting down her bundle of bitter herbs for the coming Passover.

On exactly the first day of the first month of the second year since they had left Egypt, the whole camp celebrated the Passover. This time there was no fear of the dark night outside, no anxious thoughts about the morning, the flight to freedom.

Joy filled the tent as the solemn ceremony was performed. Tirzah did not bother to hide her tears when Oren said the prepared words in answer to their father's question: "Do you know the meaning of this night?"

Proudly Tirzah held the newest member of the family on

her lap and whispered, "See, this is your family. Aren't you glad?"

After the Passover days ended, there were more lessons. Abihail rarely waited for Tirzah these days. From the corner of her eye Tirzah saw her red-gold head bent together with a group of older girls, all of whom were of marriageable age and talked of nothing else.

"Hi. Waiting for someone?" Ephan, cheerful as usual, caught up with Tirzah.

"No, just thinking," Tirzah replied. Now that she had the chance, there was something she wanted to ask Ephan. "Mind if I walk with you?"

Ephan's round face looked pleased. "I need the company," she said.

For a while they walked in silence. Tirzah was in no hurry, and Ephan didn't seem to be, either.

"Ephan, I did want to ask you something," Tirzah said. "How did you do that this morning? I mean, you were the only one who had those long commandments down perfectly." Her own attempt to recite them had been painfully poor.

Shyly Ephan glanced at Tirzah. "If you really want to know," she said, "it was easy. I made it all into a little song last night so I could remember it."

Tirzah grinned. The idea was a good one. "Ephan, do you think I could learn that way, too?"

"Why don't you try?" Ephan offered, her eyes alight with pleasure. They walked as far as they could together, Ephan singing the lines, and Tirzah repeating them.

At the parting of the path, Tirzah reluctantly went on alone. She liked Ephan. How was it that she hadn't known that before? The fact that the girl worked like a son for her father and seemed shy didn't mean anything. She was strong; that was something. And she was keen, and her voice was really rich and sweet.

As she passed the doorway of Jerioth's tent, Merrie, a

cheerful smile on her face, waved to her. The fever had left her weak. Tirzah knew that she still mourned for Hanna, though she never complained.

Some people still slighted Merrie because she was Egyptian. Tirzah's chin went up resolutely—no one would say a word against Merrie while she was around. She waved back heartily.

Nahaloth and Maacah had come to see the baby. Nahaloth picked Deborah up and held her in her arms. Maacah kneeled by them cooing and clucking like a mother bird. Tirzah was the envy of both girls since the youngest in their household was eleven years old.

When Deborah squeezed her eyes shut and began to wail loudly, her mother took her from Nahaloth's arms with a sigh.

"Time to nurse again. One of these days, you will have your own babe to care for," she said, looking directly at Nahaloth. "Or do the rumors I hear count for nothing?"

Nahaloth blushed. "What can I say, Aunt Leah? You know how people talk." Nahaloth was the oldest girl, already of marriageable age. The matchmakers lost no time trying to find suitors as soon as a girl was ready, and Nahaloth was no exception.

Tirzah grinned, thinking of the work the aunts would make of it, and all the while Nahaloth had eyes for only one—Haran, son of Peleg. But so far, Haran, the hunter, seemed to care for nothing but his bow, sharpening his arrows, and hunting. How in the world would he ever marry someone like Nahaloth, who was so squeamish? Tirzah had seen her retch at the sight of a dead coney covered with flies.

The sudden sound of the trumpets silenced them all. It lasted for several minutes—clear, high notes filling the air, then dying away to stillness. Tirzah looked at her mother, who nodded.

"Yes, it's the call to prepare for the march. We are moving

again," she said. "Come, there is much to do." Nahaloth and Maacah left hastily, and Tirzah followed her mother inside.

She went first to the rock Benj had given her, wrapped it closely inside her best clothes, and began packing. So, Nahaloth would escape the aunts for a while longer. A thought entered her mind and found its way to her lips. "Mother, when Ram is ready to marry, do you think Merrie will be the one?"

Her mother's back stiffened. Her voice was unsteady. "What gave you such an idea?" Before Tirzah could answer, she went on. "The girl is a good enough girl, but she has no family, no background. She is also a full-blooded Egyptian."

"But she loves Yahweh," Tirzah protested. "And now that Jerioth has taken her to live with them, she really isn't alone anymore."

Her mother turned to face her with flashing eyes. "I don't know what puts such things in your head. I don't want to hear another word about it. When the time comes, Ram's wife will be chosen."

Tirzah was quick to see the shadow of pain—or was it something else—that passed over her mother's face?

It isn't fair, she thought. What if I'd been Merrie and it was me Ram loved? She knew how her brother looked at Merrie, how Merrie brightened whenever he was near. Tirzah stopped packing as the thought struck her—she was match-making. Was that to be her destiny? Tirzah, the match-maker?

20

Hard Lessons

In the night sky, stars hung so low and large it looked to
Tirzah as if she could almost touch them. She could make
out the belt of the hunter with its small jewels linking the
larger ones down to the smallest one.

Tirzah sighed and wished for the sleep that usually came
too soon to her. She shut her eyes, but the stars shone behind them, turning suddenly to stones, falling from the sky.
Quickly she opened them. Would she never forget?

Again she saw the valley, the stones covering the boy's
body. The boy's mother was an Israelite, his father an Egyptian. In a fight with one of the Israelites, he had blasphemed
the name of Yahweh.

For days they had kept him under guard until Yahweh
spoke his will to Moses: "If anyone curses his God, he will
answer with his life." Had he died quickly? They had
thrown so many stones.

Tirzah was so sorry for his mother. No one spoke openly
of the boy, though there was much grumbling in the camp
about many things. Tirzah shivered at the thought of Yahweh's anger. She remembered Ram's words.

"In Egypt, to curse the Pharaoh brought death, a slow, tortured death," Ram said. "We all knew this. Doesn't Yahweh's name deserve more honor than the Pharaoh's? His words are just and must be obeyed."

It's true, Tirzah thought, but still she was afraid. The stars looking down at her were as bright as ever, only now sleep came unannounced, making her heavy eyelids close.

On the following day the air was like a furnace, the ground baked, and Tirzah had no energy to spare. Helping to set up, take down, fetch water, and scrounge for food to add to the daily manna seemed to take all her time. Days were long, nights short. It was too hot to sing or joke. Only Abishur still managed to play his flute.

Now Tirzah was furious. Arms crossed, she stood her ground under the midday sun. Abihail's face was untroubled, her blue eyes feigned innocence. "Abihail, you can't mean it," Tirzah stormed. "How can you suddenly turn away from Abishur? How could you let that wolf of a brother take his place? Your father would never force you to do such a thing."

"He isn't making me, silly," Abihail retorted. "Jonathan is a man with property and a leader. I have nothing against Abishur, of course. He will be dear to me as always, but Jonathan is older, more mature," she said.

She tossed one thick, red braid behind her shoulder to join the other. "Everyone agrees that a betrothal before we get to Canaan is best. Jonathan thinks so, too."

Tirzah stamped her foot. "Abishur is worth ten Jonathans, and you know it."

Abihail's eyes flashed. "Don't be so childish. I don't know why I bother with you. Let me know when you grow up." She turned swiftly and left Tirzah staring and open-mouthed.

Abihail was little more than a year and a half older than Tirzah. Tears filled her eyes, and she brushed them away. A part of her life was gone. Things between them would never be the same. And Abishur, what about him?

The heat continued worse than ever. Like dull thunder, rumblings of discontent rolled through the camp. Some of the worst grumblers went about loudly demanding that something be done. Some shook their fists at the name of Moses.

Tirzah wanted to close her ears to the complaints that grew daily for meat to eat instead of the same old manna. It frightened her to hear shouts of "life was better in Egypt than here in this desert."

What if their open defiance brought Yahweh's judgment on the whole camp? Late into the night Tirzah listened to the low voices of her uncle Caleb, Molid, and her father. There was fear now of mutiny.

Her worst fears came with the flocks of quail. The birds flew in low, like a storm of dark-winged wind, wave after wave, dropping down to rest from their long flight. The ground was covered with them within a day's walk around the camp.

All day and night and the day following, people gathered the quail. Tirzah and Oren worked until their arms ached. It did not occur to Tirzah that Yahweh was angry until the next day.

Abishur stood breathless in the tent doorway. "Aunt Leah, can you help us?" His hair was uncombed, his face gray with tiredness.

"It's Jonathan and our mother." Tirzah's mother stared blankly at him. "Haven't you heard?" he cried, "The plague is upon us."

For weeks there was meat to eat, but Tirzah hated the sight of the roasted quail. Yahweh had sent the meat the people demanded, but his anger followed swiftly. Many who ate greedily, forgetting about Yahweh, lay silent now in their graves because of the plague. Jonathan, who hated

Moses and blamed him for his father's death, was among those stricken.

During the funeral for Jonathan, Tirzah shivered at her father's words: "This place is now called Kibroth Hattaavah, the Graves of Craving."

When the others left, she lingered by the graveside with Abishur. Her heart was heavy for him, fatherless and now brotherless.

Abishur was pale and weary from the long night watch. He raised his flute one more time in a lonely farewell song to part of him that lay in the desert, soon to be left behind.

As the notes rose, mournful, fainting, and rising again, Tirzah saw through her tears that Ephan had come to stand beside her. For a moment, she hoped that Abihail too would come. But Tirzah had seen her leave, leaning on the arm of her father, widowed before her marriage. Ephan held Tirzah's hand in her own large, comforting hand, and together they wept as Abishur played.

• • •

The sickness passed quickly, and once more they were marching toward the Promised Land. Out of sight of the place of graves, Tirzah felt lighter, as if a heavy burden was no longer sitting on her shoulders. At Hazeroth, Yahweh's cloud stood still, marking the new campsite. Tirzah unpacked her treasures and set the fish stone from Benj in its position of honor. After that she rocked Deborah in her arms until the baby fell asleep.

Leah watched her growing daughter with approval. Tirzah was lean but stronger than ever, the muscles of her legs hard as rock, her eyes bright. A glow of pride filled Leah. Tirzah would make a good wife and mother one day. Unaware of her mother's thoughts, Tirzah rocked baby Deborah in her arms, singing softly to her about the land of milk and honey they would soon see.

"I think she already loves the Promised Land," she said. "Look how she smiles even in sleep." Leah smiled at both her daughters.

In Jerioth's tent the sudden stillness of the night was broken by a cry from Merrie, awakened from sleep. Cold sweat ran down her back and her eyes were full of some half-forgotten dream. Jerioth soothed the girl's trembling, brushing the thick, damp hair from her forehead and whispering words of comfort to her.

When Jerioth lay down once again close to Molid's side to snuggle into her husband's warmth, he mumbled, "Is she all right?"

"Yes, she seems to be quiet now," Jerioth replied, her voice low. "But Molid, what is to become of the child? People are so cruel, my husband. Can you imagine blaming the girl for being Egyptian? She is more uncomplaining, more faithful to Yahweh, than the very ones who spurn her. It makes me mad."

Molid grunted. "She is safe enough with us. Once we get to the Promised Land, you'll find her a husband." He rolled over on his stomach. "Besides, I think that young Ram has his eye on her."

Jerioth smiled. Ram was a good boy, like his father. The lad had grown up during their travels. Yes, that was a real possibility. Still, Leah would not be keen about having an Egyptian daughter-in-law. Why was she so set against the girl? Jerioth closed her eyes and let her thoughts drift. Tomorrow, she would try to talk to Leah.

• • •

Leah was not in a listening mood. She handed Deborah to Jerioth while she searched for a coin that had fallen from her necklace. The bright silver piece rolled itself into a corner just out of reach. She seized her broom and swept it out.

"It isn't that I have anything against the girl," she said, picking up the coin. "But I want Ram to marry one of his own, someone who has roots to share with him, you know." Leah took the baby from Jerioth. "Let's not talk about it anymore. Anyway, who is in a hurry about these things, eh?" she said. Gently she touched Deborah's tiny rosebud mouth, which immediately tried to fasten on her finger.

Shaking her head, Jerioth turned away from Leah. Some things wouldn't wait, she thought, but what else could she do now?

As if reading her thoughts, Leah added, "Yesterday I heard that even Miriam and Aaron are angry with Moses because of his foreign wife. Have you heard the rumors?" She didn't pause for Jerioth's answer, but went on. "They're saying that Aaron and Miriam have just as much right to lead as Moses, maybe more. His wife is not a Hebrew, after all, and you see what trouble it causes."

So that's it, Jerioth thought, turning to face Leah. "I can't think for a moment that the man chosen by Yahweh to lead us from Egypt, the one to whom he gave the commandments, does not please him," she said.

Jerioth's tone softened as she pleaded for Merrie. "Leah, my dear friend, we've gone through so much together, but in just this one thing I cannot agree with you. We must not forget that Yahweh promised to make our ancestor Abraham a father of many nations, to bless many through his descendants. Will you or I cut off one who chooses to love and follow Yahweh?"

Jerioth's eyes were full of tears. "If Yahweh accepts Moses' wife and Merrie as well, mustn't we?"

Leah was still for a long moment. "I can accept the girl," she half-whispered, "but Ram must marry within his own people." No more was said till Tirzah ran breathlessly into the tent, her face white as the broom flower.

"Mother, it's Miriam, they've turned her out of the camp." Tirzah stood still, her heart pounding. "Maacah and I were near the Tent of Meeting. We saw a crowd gathering and ran to see what was happening. It was terrible, terrible."

Tirzah could not control the sobs that bathed her face with tears and choked her words. "She was snow-white—a leper, her hands, her face, all that we could see."

A look of horror washed over Leah's face. "But why, but how?" she stuttered.

"Oh, Mother, Yahweh has punished her for speaking against Moses." Tirzah's words fell like a knife into Leah's heart. Without a word she handed Deborah to Tirzah and went quickly from the tent, followed by Jerioth.

For three days, her mother mourned, eating nothing, drinking only a little water. The baby cried for what seemed like hours on end. Tirzah rocked her, held her, walked her, but nothing helped. On the third day, her father put his foot down.

Tall and muscular, he stood with both feet planted solidly in the tent doorway. His black eyes took in the scene unchanged for the last three days. "Tirzah, fetch a bowl of stew for your mother," he roared.

Tirzah hurried to obey him. From outside the tent, she could hear his booming voice.

"Enough, Leah, I have had enough. You don't eat, the baby doesn't eat. You will eat, do you hear me? I won't have you upsetting the household like this for two whole weeks while Miriam suffers her just punishment."

He leaned down and drew his wife to her feet. "Now, woman, Yahweh has said that in two weeks her leprosy will be taken away. Can't you be patient?"

Her mother fell sobbing into his arms. "Oh, Jeraheel, what of me? I too was guilty of her sin," she sobbed.

Tirzah stood stricken in the doorway, her mother's food held stiffly in one hand. What was her mother saying?

"I sinned, Jeraheel. I too spoke against Moses' wife." Her mother's words cut into Tirzah's chest. "Oh, my husband, I did not want to think of our Ram marrying an Egyptian girl, and I was angry."

Her father's voice was full of astonishment. "You mean that you would not consider Merrie?" he asked. "A girl who has left all to follow Yahweh, who risked her life to be faithful to him?"

"Yes, oh, yes," Leah cried. "I am guilty, guilty." She was almost unable to stand and sank weakly against his chest.

For a long moment there was silence. "We will go to Aaron with an offering. It will be all right, my love. Hush, hush now." His big hands stroked her hair gently. "We have all learned much on this journey. Yahweh is merciful."

Tirzah swallowed hard. If only her mother could see Ram's eyes brighten at the sound of Merrie's voice, or watch Merrie's face as Ram taught her the stories of Yahweh, she would love her.

On the day after Miriam's cure, when the whole camp moved on to the desert of Paran, Ram asked his mother to arrange for his betrothal to Merrie. With a long quiet look, his mother gave her assent.

Tirzah, dancing for joy, ran to tell Ephan. "Promise me, Ephan, promise me that you will sing at the celebration," she begged.

Ephan blushed, making her cheery face quite pretty, but she promised. "But remember," she said, "you must stand next to me all the while."

When he heard the news, Oren threw his crutch into the air, narrowly missing the waterpot, and whooped loudly. "I am to be brother-in-law to Paser's niece, and she makes the best ink and parchment around."

Laughing, Jeraheel retrieved Oren's crutch for him, inspecting it with a critical eye before handing it back. "I think it's time we made you a new crutch, son," he said.

"I want to wait, father." Oren answered quietly. A puzzled silence filled the tent, and all eyes turned to Oren expectantly. "This one has come a long way with me. I'd rather wait till we reach the new land for another."

"Let it be so, son," Jeraheel said.

"Amen," Leah added.

"Amen," whispered Tirzah.

21

A Song of Hope

Kadesh was a good place for the camp. Tirzah knelt by a little spring and splashed its cold, clear water on her face, then her arms. Sitting back on her heels, she listened to its burbling rush around the stones sticking above the water. The sound of running water was a good sound, one she would never forget. Her own waterskin was full, and Ephan was nearly finished filling hers.

"Ephan, are you ever afraid?" Tirzah suddenly asked. "I mean, do you think we will have to fight the Canaanites the way we fought the Amalekites? Moses says that Yahweh will drive out the people of the land before us. I know he will, but Ram says we must fight, too." Tirzah sat still thinking of the last war, the only war she had seen so far.

Ephan lifted her waterskin, her broad face thoughtful. "Maybe both Ram and Moses are right. Yahweh alone fought the Egyptians for us," she said.

"I know," Tirzah interrupted, "but we fought the Amalekites." Hastily she added, "And Yahweh gave us victory, if that's what you mean."

As they walked, Ephan said in a gentle voice, "You asked

153

me if I ever feel afraid. Sometimes at night I think about what could happen. Another raid, or worse, a mutiny in the camp. That scares me more."

She sighed. "Some people turn away from following Yahweh over the least hard thing. I'm not very brave, but one lesson I learned from my father—stick to the job, whatever it is. I can't help it; I just plod ahead. The hard jobs sometimes turn out to be the ones that make you feel best about yourself when the thing's done."

What Ephan said made sense, and Tirzah nodded. "You're strong, Ephan. I just want to get to the Promised Land as fast as we can."

The path narrowed, forcing them to go single file past an outcrop of rocks on either side.

"It can't be too much longer, Tiz," Ephan said. "The men Moses sent to spy out the land should be coming back soon."

Tirzah balanced her waterskin carefully until she was on flat ground once more. "My father is anxious for Uncle Caleb to come back with the news."

The men had been gone for almost a month. No one knew if they were safe or not. She was proud that her favorite uncle was one of the twelve men chosen to spy out the land of Canaan. But why weren't they back? People were beginning to worry.

Aloud she said, "When there's a job to do, Uncle Caleb's like your father; he just keeps on till it's done." At least she hoped so.

Tirzah and Ephan were hardly back when the news came. "They've come, they've come," the shout rang through the camp. From every direction people dropped what they were doing and ran.

The men had returned. Tirzah snatched a glimpse of her uncle among them as they passed. Like the rest, his clothes were stained, his face dirty and tired. Before she could wave, they were swallowed up in a rush of people. At the Tent of Meeting, the crowds waited for word. Tirzah stood with her mother next to Jerioth and her family to hear the news passed from tribe to tribe.

The report began well. "A good land, flowing with milk and honey," the word came down. "You should see the size of the grapes—big and sweet, like these we brought to show you. The pomegranates, too—wonderful. Good soil, well watered."

Tirzah was almost dizzy with joy. But what was this they were saying now?

"Walled cities and people so large they made us look like grasshoppers. Descendants of the Anak, a race of giants. Amalekites living there as well. The people are too strong for us."

Tirzah stood frozen at the words. Then, like the strong man that he was, she heard her uncle Caleb's voice roaring above the rest. "There is no need to fear. Listen to Moses. We can take possession of the land. We are well able to overcome it."

Young Joshua stood by her uncle, adding his plea to Caleb's. It was useless. Not one of the other ten spies agreed with them.

The decision of the others was firm: "We can't attack those people. They are stronger than we are." Women tore their clothes, and men shook their fists at Moses and Aaron. Some wailed, and others shouted in anger.

The crowds were getting out of hand. In the confusion, Jeraheel pushed and elbowed to drag his family to safety. For an instant Tirzah lost sight of her father, then Ram was pulling her by the arm out of the crush of the crowd. Panic made her heart beat faster as Ram led her through the chaos.

Free of the crowds at last, they reached the tents safely. Then her father returned with Ram and Molid to help Caleb.

It was a day like none Tirzah had seen since their flight

from the Egyptian army. In the tent her mother lay on the ground weeping and moaning. Baby Deborah, worn out with crying, slept in her bed. For once, Jerioth, the beautiful, cheerful Jerioth, could comfort no one. She too lay face down upon the ground in her tent, weeping quietly.

There was no one to turn to. Tirzah's legs felt weak, her whole body numb. She sat down in the tent doorway where she could see and wait. What she was waiting for, she didn't know.

After a while, she thought to look up and see if Yahweh's cloud was still above the tabernacle. It was. Yahweh was still with them. Yahweh is giving us the Promised Land, she thought. He can do it. Uncle Caleb and Joshua said so, too.

Her mother's sobs still came from the tent periodically, and finally Tirzah rose and went to her.

"It will be all right, Mother," she crooned. "Listen, Uncle Caleb knows." Her mother made no response, her face still buried in her arms. In her corner of the tent, baby Deborah slept peacefully.

"Mother, remember the Song of Moses?" Tirzah began to hum it, then to sing, "Horse and rider he has hurled into the sea."

Her mother lifted her head at last, her large eyes full of sorrow. "Not this time, little bird. Yahweh is angry with us for our sins," she said haltingly. With a sudden rush of fear, she clutched Tirzah to her fiercely. "I cannot bear to see you die," she wailed.

When her mother's grip loosened a little, Tirzah pleaded with her, rocking with her like a child. "Mother, Mother, I'm not going to die. Yahweh is still with us. Have you forgotten his cloud? Come and see it, Mother, please."

Leah only covered her eyes, shaking her head. "No, little one, not this time. Don't you see? Many have died under Yahweh's cloud. He is angry with us, angry with us." Tirzah could get nowhere with her mother.

By evening the crowds, who had listened all day to the words of the ten men, were ready to stone Moses.

"We want a new leader," one cried, and the refrain was picked up and repeated. Others shouted for a return to Egypt. "The Canaanites will take our wives and our children," someone screamed.

The entire camp was assembled to listen and decide what to do. Tirzah stood once more by her trembling mother, who leaned heavily against Jeraheel. Moses and Aaron lay on their faces before the people. Once more Caleb and Joshua tried to appeal to the crowds.

"Do not rebel against the Lord," her uncle was crying out. "If Yahweh is pleased with us, he will give us this land. Do not be afraid of the people. Their protection is gone, but the Lord is with us."

Tirzah wanted to cheer her uncle's words, shout Yahweh's name, but the muttering crowds frightened her, and her voice barely whispered, "The Lord is with us."

"People are picking up stones," Ram said. "They'll stone Moses and Aaron, Caleb and Joshua. No!" he shouted.

Almost at the same time, the cloud of Glory seemed to swell with burning fire at the Tent of Meeting. Someone cried, "Look, look, Yahweh's glory." The crowds hushed to a silence so thick Tirzah could feel it. She trembled as if with fever. Would Yahweh's anger strike them all?

Moses entered the tabernacle while the people stood waiting. It seemed to Tirzah the most awful moment of her life. Every eye turned toward him when he reappeared. With halting steps Moses walked from the tabernacle to face the people. Tears streamed down his face as he brought them Yahweh's words. Tirzah felt her own heart breaking.

"Yahweh's love and mercy are great," Moses began in a choked voice that grew stronger as he continued. "He forgives sin and rebellion, yet he does not leave the guilty unpunished."

From bowed head to bowed head, a sigh rose like one breath above the people. "Only Caleb and Joshua," Moses went on, "and the children you said would be taken as plunder, will enter the Promised Land."

A murmur like a great gasp broke from the listeners.

"Wait," Moses cried out, "there is more. Only those under the age of twenty will enter the land. But you and your children shall wander as shepherds in the desert for forty years until only the children remain, and then they shall enter the land." In a stillness as deathly as that of a mass funeral, the people went quietly to their tents. No one argued, no one protested, no one spoke to a neighbor.

They lit no fire that night, but sat in a little family group— her father, mother, Ram, Oren, small Deborah, Abishur, and herself. Tirzah could not speak for grief. With a burning lump in her throat, she listened to her father. Tears rolled down his face as he prayed.

When he was through, he held his wife's hand in his own large one. "My children," he said, "though we shall never see the good land Yahweh has promised, you will."

He paused for strength, then went on. "Your mother and I will prepare you for the day that will come when you shall enter the land. You will take our places, be our eyes, our ears. Your joy will be for us too."

Tirzah could hardly bear the pain in her heart as he continued. "We shall teach you all that we can, my dear ones, for as long as Yahweh wills.

"Remember, my dear," he patted his weeping wife's shoulder, "we are forgiven. Yahweh's love is great and his decree is just. He will care for us all our days here in the desert. Always, we can look up and see his cloud of Glory with us." Her mother nodded, unable to speak.

"And though we die here in the desert, our lives can be good ones, eh?" He lifted his hands high for a silent moment.

From somewhere the words of the Song of Moses made their way to Tirzah's lips. "Sing to the Lord for he has risen up in triumph: horse and rider he has hurled into the sea," she whispered.

Abishur began to play his flute, and backed by the music, Tirzah's voice grew stronger. One by one the others joined them, singing with voices still heavy with pain, but behind the pain—hope.

The Author

Lucille Travis, free-lance writer, lives in Arden Hills, Minnesota, with her husband, William, a church history professor at Bethel Seminary. She has a degree in Bible from Gordon College and a master's degree in literature from Western Connecticut State University.

Lucille has taught English at the college level and lectured in Christian fantasy and literature in schools and local churches. Currently she is involved in tutoring Hmong women in English as a second language.

Her first book for children, *A Summer's Growth,* was published by Baker Book House in 1982. It is set in Tarrytown, New York (her native state), where the Travises and their three children, Phil, Chris, and Bryan, lived for seventeen years. Her poetry, articles, and reviews have appeared in Christian publications over the years. An example is her story for children in the February 1989 issue of *Focus on the Family Clubhouse Magazine.*

Lucille is a member of the Salem Baptist Church, New Brighton, Minnesota.